D1356399

TURKISH DELIGHT

RASTAPOULOS *Me? Bad? Of course I'm bad! I'm the devil incarnate...that's what I am. And let's hear anyone try to deny it!*

CARREIDAS *I beg your pardon! I am the devil incarnate... and I'm richer than you are, too!*

RASTAPOULOS *So what? Listen to this! I ruined my three brothers and two sisters, and dragged my parents into the gutter. What d'you say to that, eh?*

CARREIDAS *Peanuts! Kid's stuff! My great-aunt was so ashamed of me she lay down and died! Beat that!*

RASTAPOULOS *Now let's get this straight. Yes or no! Do you or do you not admit that I'm wickeder than you?*

CARREIDAS *Never!...Never, d'you hear?...I'd sooner die!*

The Adventures of Tintin
Flight 714

TURKISH DELIGHT

Jan Wolkers

Translated from the Dutch

by

Greta Kilburn

CALDER & BOYARS

LONDON

First published in Great Britain in 1974 by Calder &
Boyars Ltd, 18 Brewer Street London W 1R 4 AS

First published in Dutch in 1969
by Meulenhoff, Amsterdam

ISBN 0 7145 1055 6 Casebound Edition

Set in Baskerville by Thomson Press (India) Limited,
New Delhi-1, and printed by The Pitman Press,
Bath, England.

CONTENTS

Chicory and Whiskers

I was in a pretty awful mess after she left me. I didn't work any more, I didn't eat any more. I lay between my dirty sheets all day and stuck up nude pictures of her by my face so I could imagine her long pasted eyelashes moving as I jacked off. And watch her lips grow full and curl out, damp, and hear the cries as she came, noisy like in the beginning when she hadn't learned yet to keep the pleasure between her and me and would have yelled it to the whole world, so that the woman next door asked her: "What's he doing to you?" And a neighbour said to me: "You must be keeping a litter of pups in there". I read her letters again and copied out sentences on the wall: AFTER I LEFT YOU I HAD TO RUN INTO THE CHEMIST FOR COTTONWOOL TO STOP THE BLEEDING OF MY HEART. And: HERE IN THE CITY YOU COULD SMELL THE HAY LAST NIGHT. I LONG FOR YOU. AS I WRITE MY CUNT IS MAKING SUCKING MOTIONS LIKE A BABY'S MOUTH. I racked my brains trying to figure out what had gone wrong, why she had left me for such a drip, a salesman, an overgrown prick with sagging shoulders. The skin on my head began to ache from thinking and agonizing. I couldn't make it out, I just couldn't understand. How could she have let herself be poisoned like that. It was that stinking bitch of a mother of hers. Then I'd jack off again beside that picture of her, naked, sitting with her back turned. She raises herself just a bit so that her bum hangs down heavily. And I called out, have a shit, goddammit, shit for me, and I'll lick your arse clean. But after a fortnight I'd had enough and got out of bed. Thin and filthy. In the kitchen I found the last thing she had done in the house. In a frying pan on the gas stove. Two meat balls. They were lying in a downy bed of mildew and when I flushed them down the toilet I could have laughed and cried at the same time because I remembered the meat ball she had sent to the Food Inspection Department when she was at boarding school. I took a shower and rubbed myself raw with the skeleton of a sea cucumber that had her red hairs wound round it like nylon thread. I put on my best clothes and studied myself intently in the mirror. With my thin face and wild curls, my tight black trousers and black leather jacket I thought that I looked immortally beautiful. And I whispered to myself in all seriousness, because I couldn't laugh about it: "Some of your luck still holds." I reacted just like that little jew in the joke who gets caught by a friend coming out of a whorehouse on the day of his wife's funeral and says: "So with a grief like mine, I should know what I'm doing?" I screwed one bird after another. I dragged them to my lair, tore the clothes off them, rammed myself silly, then got rid of them after a quick drink. Up to three in one day. Big tits hanging like sacks of mush with nipples ripe for sucking. Small shrivelled tits,

8

too pathetic to stroke. Not worth taking her sweater off for. Shocks of pubic hair, rough as seaweed, soft as fur. Dry cunts with warts inside. Queer on the fingers, but nice on your cock. Cunts you didn't get to see because a little hand shielded them. Cunts soft and damp as a custard bun. Strapping birds with hips like cheeses and a Rotterdam accent full of aggression who held your prick like it was the handle of a drill. They wanted to do the dishes and mop the floor and scrub the can the minute the screwing was over. Girls who put a wet nose in the hair of your chest and wept because they'd been raped by their father when they were fifteen. The Indonesian who did the maiden trip and called out in half-assed, half-rounded tones: "What are you doing with me?" "I'm opening your thighs and I'm poking my prick in you and I'm going to fuck you till I can't smell that sweet breath of yours any more. Come on with your sticky lips. Let your tongue hang out and I'll eat it up." The stinking headache it gave me to wake up and find another pad at the head of my mattress. The blood a browny black, like treacle. The crabs they brought you, grey scales on your skin with the greetings of many friends from far-off countries. And I noted all these brief encounters in a diary. Often with a lock of hair glued in the margin, pubic hair if they'd been fool enough. And how I had seduced them or sometimes how they had seduced me. And what they had said, and what I had said. Because nothing is so appealing to a woman as a man who suffers from a lost love. But after a few months it made me puke. I slowed down a bit, let my sitting room to a couple of American girls and didn't lay a hand on either of them. They were studying art history and between a reproduction of Memlinc's *Lamb of God* and the inevitable self-portrait of that

9

lunatic in Arles with a bandage around his nut they had pinned proverbs on the wall: THERE IS NOTHING SADDER THAN ASSOCIATIONS HELD TOGETHER BY NOTHING BUT THE GLUE OF POSTAGE STAMPS. And: HE WHO PUTS SALT IN THE SUGAR BOWL IS A MISAN-THROPE. Every Friday they returned from the market with a slimy newspaper full of miserable little plaice even though they weren't Catholics. They salted them in the sink, which was slippery from the gobbing and pissing I did in it and stank of rotten lettuce. They were too stupid to use a plate. That's why I didn't say anything the time they put chicory on the gas in my shaving pot and I could see the rim of soap caked with black hairs slowly melt into the boiling vegetables. It wouldn't have helped. Anyhow, they said in America everything tasted of soap, which is probably why they took a shower four times a day. The shower was right over the toilet so I could hear them splash and giggle when I spread myself out on the can to read the paper. And because they frequent-ly sat on the drain the water came down through the cracks. At first the walls just got damp, but after a few months I counted seven different kinds of fungus. Then chalk-like bulges began to grow out from the wall and the ceiling so that it looked as if their vaginal flora was seeding itself through the floor like grubby coral. I said nothing about that either, taking into account that I used the shower too. Every other day by agreement. I came into their room in my under-wear. They sat on the divan with their perky American noses deep in the books. Spelling Dutch out loud. From the Catacombs to El Greco and all that shit. Then I took off my shorts and undershirt and threw them in a pile on the floor. I suspected them of trying to get a swift peep at my arse before my hairy body disappeared into the shower. And then quickly continue to read to each other about Giotto and Cimabue or some of those other old farts. If I was in a good mood I'd stick my head out of the door and roar: "Rembrandt is the greatest bungler of the seventeenth century." They tensed then and didn't dare look my way because they didn't know what was sticking through the door. Then I turned on the tap while I loudly sang The Star-Spangled Banner. Once in the lukewarm water holding my stiff cock in my hand I imagined that I would walk into their room, lie between them and be jacked off cool and hard with those eager grab-dollar hands. They would grease my belly with the seed and paste stamps in it steamed off letters from America with pictures of the Statue of Liberty with IN GOD WE TRUST over it and LIBERTY below. Or with pictures of one of their historical old fogeys, a toothless old bag in light green or pale purple from their glorious past of Indian, buffalo, negro and brother murder. But it never happened. In the beginning they protested my naked state when entering and leaving the shower. I didn't even answer them. I went downstairs, laid my prick on the side of the table on a piece of paper, drew a line around it, wrote MY PENIS above it and pushed it under their door. I didn't see it hanging among their reproductions and proverbs nor was it in the dustbin. So I suspect that one of them walks around to this very day with it stuck like a jewel between her skin and her unsavoury panties. They put an American boy they'd got to know in the city on to me though. A chubby one with a crew cut and the appearance of a teddy bear but with vicious pale eyes. He called in his official capacity as Elder of the Church of Jesus Christ of the Latter-Day Saints. They had probably shown him my drawing and he wanted to start the conversion off by returning that erection to its simple state under the motto: My Redeemer hangs on the Cross. At least he began by giving me a card with a colour photo of a weird building guarding a temple dome resembling a warped egg. The Latter-Day Saints temple in Salt Lake City, Utah. When he wanted to deliver a sermon on the Book of Mormon I reminded him that Americans are not religious at all. That they only think in hard dollars. That surely he must know that Mormon was short for More Money. He shook his head and stayed calm. Because you can't begin by throwing napalm. But when he took three small figures from his pocket and set them on the table like chess pieces and introduced them as the holy apostles Peter, John and James, I couldn't resist opening my fly, producing my cock and saying: "And this is the holy Habakkuk." He left with much shaking of the head and mild regret for the loss of a customer. He did manage to snatch the three holy apostles from my table as if they were small change. I never saw him again. But I saw plenty of their other boyfriends. Pale American students roaming around the continent on grants too small to live on but too big to starve. So they wandered restlessly through a no man's land of indeterminate girls' rooms, the deep pockets of their frayed army coats full of popcorn, chewing gum and pumpernickel. From Stavanger to Naples. When I went for a shower one morning I counted fifteen of them. They were spread around the floor wrapped in grey horse blankets or pieces of Indian cloth, asleep or slowly ruminating on a strawberry jam sandwich. I picked my way through the room as if they were a colony of seals. Careful not to tread on tails or flippers. If one of them had a guitar they sang folksongs all afternoon sometimes with such fervour that the neighbours phoned and asked me to turn the radio down. When I asked the girls if maybe they wouldn't like to have an affair with one of these boys because I hoped that the rest would then sound the retreat, they seemed fussy. It turned out that one was "too hot to handle", and another "chewed his gum too loud". So things went on with sleepers on the hard floor, eaters and showerers. The stalactites on the ceiling of my toilet grew at an alarming rate, fed with bacteria, dandruff and crusts from all the fifty states of America. When they took in a dozen parakeets and let them fly freely about the room so that when I came out of the shower the feathered shit got stuck between my toes and I doubled up with pain from the sharp birdseed pressing into my soles, my cup overflowed. I kicked Uncle Sam's clochards out, flung open the windows and drove the parakeets into the street with the rugbeater like I was playing a game of badminton. I yelled to the pale and sobbing girls who were trying to catch the parakeets with tulle head scarves among the bushes in front of the house that they could fuck off with their popcorn and sweet potatoes; that I was giving them notice right now, before their rotten birds had nibbled all four walls of the room down to the fucking frame with their fucking crooked beaks. The same afternoon they caused a brief commotion in the street when they wheeled away their belongings on a pushcart with about ten of their boyfriends in tow, each carrying a couple of parakeets in nets purchased hastily in a nearby fishing-gear shop. They even came to shake my hand. Sickening. They could have at least reproached me for forgetting the Marshall Plan. Or thrown the proverb at me they'd left on the wall in the shambles of their room: HE WHO PUTS SALT IN THE SUGARBOWL IS A MISANTHROPE.

13

The Wings of Hermes

I knew that the underside of the tubby little chair where he always sat was a miniature mountain-scape of dried snot. He plumbed it out of his nose with his little finger, forged it into little balls which he called bullets and pressed these carefully against the bottom of his chair. It was one of the first things she told me about him because she adored her father. It mortified her mother when the help discovered it during the spring cleaning. The woman first thought it was glue or resin and tried to pick it off with her nails. But even with the breadknife only a few flakes would chip off, so they had to leave those yellowy green reliefs where they were. There were mountains more to come anyway. You couldn't break his habits. He might be good natured but he was like a wilful child when it came to his snot. At meals he always folded his lettuce before eating it, otherwise the lice might run away. And when they played the "Radetzky March" on the radio, he accompanied it with: "Titty bum, titty bum, titty bum, bum, bum, Titty bum, titty bum, titty bum, bum, bum." Keeping time. Not when his wife was in the room of course. Once, when Olga was a little girl, she had thrown up all over the dinner table and burst into tears. Her mother was disgusted and left the table, but he took one of her teddy bears and kept bending it over the vomit while saying: "Poor bear sick. Poor bear sick." Until she began to laugh. I loved that man, the way he'd sit there when we came to visit, with his red blotchy face and his flabby body clamped in that chair. His fat arms puffing at his sides, at least when he wasn't making bullets. Even if he continually observed what an uncivilized people the Americans were and kept asking: "Do you know the one about the two boys who went to Paris? They didn't go." And each time he'd shake with laughter in his small tight chair. Or: "Who licks the Queen's behind?" And if you cocked your head like you were hearing it for the first time, he'd say: "Everybody who puts a stamp on a letter." And he'd go on trilling with laughter, like a pudding in an air raid. He was much too fat. He had been on a diet for years and would say: "I die for my diet". When we stayed with her parents, his wife purred around him ever so sweet and concerned. Only one wee potatoe with a touch of thin gravy. Because of his liver. He was bloody well going yellower every week. But once, after Olga and I left the table a little sooner to go and see a film and I walked back into the room to get my cigarettes, she had heaped his plate with potatoes and was lathering them with gravy. She gave me a hostile, guilty look. I had caught her at slow murder. But I didn't mention it to Olga, who would have worried without being able to do a thing about it. No one could have stopped her from fattening him up. I hated that woman. Not only for that but because she insisted on giving me motherly embraces since I was going out with her daughter, and each time I would feel the stiff cloth of an empty bra where a breast had once been. You'd go into the bathroom and find one of those newspaper-wrapped blood-birds on top of the package of clean pads. She wanted you to know that she still had what it takes. And she always came into our bedroom. To bring breakfast. A soft-boiled egg like a blubbery fart, and rusks. Staying a bit too long and sniffing around in such a lecherous way that when we were alone again, lying in the sulphurous stink of the skilfully beheaded

15

egg, I imagined her mother ripping away the blankets, sticking my prick in her daughter and saying, as she grabbed me by the balls: "I'll hang on to these." Then shaking the one breast out of her dressing gown and pushing a nipple the size of an acorn into Olga. The bitch was even then trying to turn Olga against me, and out of revenge I felt like taking her false teeth into the bathroom, locking them around my prick and jacking off into the washbasin. She met her husband in the hospital. He a patient, she a nurse. While washing, tail-rubbing and taking his temperature. She'd seen his works before he had so much as kissed her. He was shapeless, kindly and well-to-do. She was good-looking, poor, greedy and, at that time, double-breasted. A calculating woman who sneaked the afterbirths from the hospital home to her dog, a whippet whose bottom she wiped with a piece of toilet paper. She joked about her fat patient with her colleagues until they said: "Make enough fun of him and you'll end up marrying him." But she had long since decided this herself. She petted and coddled him so much that she manoeuvered him straight from the sick bed into the wedding bed. Soon she had him so fat that he was no trouble at all and could hardly move. It was all he could do to sink deep into his big American car and drive from the house to his office, a wholesale business in household goods, which, after the death of his father, he had christened Hermes. As a result of her wartime affair with a German officer, he had been able to get hold of an enormous quantity of knives very cheaply. They were left on his hands of course, as their origin was evident from the squat design and the markings, and ten years after the war he was still giving them away as presents to his customers. When he returned from puffing behind his desk all day, she often wasn't

16

home and then he wandered aimlessly through the house, calling for her like a sick, fat child. Olga came home from school to an atmosphere of sadness, despair and suspicion. He had known for a long time that at the place where she was supposed to be drinking tea with her girlfriends, she generally didn't keep her clothes on. And so it was that a family friend, who was to be addressed as "Uncle" on mother's orders, said to Olga on the beach, when she was thirteen: "Look, we have the same little toe. You're my child." The shock and bewilderment stayed with her for years. Once her father got used to his wife's affairs and resigned himself to the inevitable, he found it quite a comfortable arrangement. "She's a beautiful woman," he said, "and I'm only an albino, I cannot see too well. But drop a pin, and I hear where it falls." At times he took a little good-natured revenge. If one of her musicians or actors was on the phone and she came up to take it in her red plush slippers and a head full of curl papers, he'd say "Cauliflower speaking", just before handing it to her. Once he gave Olga a friendly slap on her backside, saying "Best watch it, I've just read in the paper that the curvy blonde is going out of fashion." Her mother looked at her jealously, as if she would have robbed her of her youth. But it made me throb. The curvy blonde. I lured Olga into the hall, shoved her into the lavatory, and did her standing. When she came, I had to pull the chain or she would have yelled the house down. But quite suddenly, it was all over with him. One morning he said his body felt just like a draining board. He went back to bed and never came out again under his own steam. When we arrived he was far gone. She finished with him as she had begun: as nurse to a fat patient. In the evening she took all the flowers out of his room and put them in the hall so that the

17

place was just like a hospital. And she walked around shaking down the thermometer with a fierce flick of the wrist, while I wondered just what she was sticking it into. By now he was a heap of blubber and the moisture was seeping through the mattress. Eau. de Cologne was sprinkled liberally throughout the house to drive away the cloying smell of decay. Olga sat nervously and aimlessly twisting a little handkerchief all day, her cheeks puffy, the whites of her big brown eyes bloodshot. At night, in bed, she lay weakly sighing in my arms, strands of wet hair sticking to her face. But it made for a nice fuck, that helpless, apathetic body. I nearly tempted her to leave off the ring, what apter place to make a baby than above a dying man? During the night she woke, crying out in her sleep and she shook me till I was awake too. I tried to console her. And then she told me, convulsed with tears, that she had been dreaming about the horse again. It was a war-time story, told them by a friend who had done forced labour in Germany. Between the Russians advancing and the Germans evacuating, he and many others like him had ended up in a Berlin suburb. No food was left in the deserted houses. They sat like rats in a trap among the rubble of a street with shells flying all around them. Suddenly a horse came into the street. They heard the clatter of his hooves on the cobbles. Everyone crowded against the broken windows and watched, speechlessly, as the animal shied his way between the stones and rubbish. All at once a door flew open and a man ran outside, grabbed the horse by the neck and tried to drag it after him. But the horse reared and fell, with the man on top of it. At that moment a second man burst out of one of the houses. The two of them cut a slice of meat out of the flank of the horse, whose piercing scream drowned out the sound of the artillery. One man after another came running out of the houses, fell on the horse and returned with a quivering piece of bloody meat. It took an hour for the screaming to stop. By then only pieces of skin and guts and bones were left, and the head of that horse with its jawful of yellow teeth was lying in an enormous pool of blood. After I had comforted her and had that horse on my own mind, she suddenly said: "My mother is a witch." Her hand flew to her mouth as if her own words terrified her. When I reminded her of it a year later, when her mother had been telling her how as an attractive widow she was being shunned by married girlfriends, she denied ever having said it. A few days later her father died. We were each allowed a brief turn to see him; I was last, being only married into the family. His face was a formless yellow mass and the watery lobes of his hanging cheeks sagging into the pillow were woven through with purple veins that ran out in red. He didn't look at me, but when I went to sit beside him he did seem to know it was me. At least he said, in a strangely high voice: "You take that red Olga of mine with you." I braced myself, for I expected a sentimental talk. That I was to take good care of his daughter, the apple of his eye. But he had too much decency for that. He said, and I thought he was trying to smile: "Do you know the one about the two boys who went to Paris?" He waited for a long time. Then, with difficulty, he said: "They didn't go." Almost inaudibly, he kept repeating "They didn't go, they didn't go, they didn't..." Then he lost consciousness. He died two hours later without having come to. From that moment the house became an hysterical cauldron. Again and again his wife stormed into his room shouting in self-reproach and remorse. She held whole conversations with him in which she asked him the same things over and over again. Then she'd change her course and come to weep around my neck, saying that I was now the head of the family. I was to give up sculpturing—that wouldn't keep a mouse alive—and become a director of Hermes. Cold terror struck my heart. I could see myself giving away those stubby German Army knives for the rest of my life. She quarrelled with the management over his cremation in Velsen, that supermarket of death. They refused to play Rezni-chek's "La Donna Diana" Overture. It wasn't solemn enough. He had been fonder of the "Radetzky March" but she didn't ask for that, as she was well aware that no one in the family could listen to it without also hearing him sing: "Titty bum, titty bum, titty bum, bum, bum." So the coffin finished up sinking through the podium to a Bach Fugue. I thought that instead of the wreaths with flowers and ribbons, that chair with all his snot should have gone ovenwards on the coffin. For that was what he'd liked best of all. A few months later when we came to see her mother who was busy organizing herself for the wintersports, the chair had disappeared. And no one knew what had become of it.

Blues for a Fur Coat

How I met her. Twice really. That red-headed witch. But I didn't call her that until after she had

20

gone off with that limp cock and when she came for her belongings—a sewing machine, a vacuum cleaner, some other pathetic bits and pieces—it appeared her eyes could flash as viciously as her mother's. But that was partly because I stood her against the mirror, wanting to do her, with her lover posted just outside for fear I might molest her. She beat back her skirt and stamped her feet like a schoolmistress. And then we both had to laugh, a little sadly. Me, because what had been so everyday for us was suddenly impossible. Why she laughed I don't know. She would have even asked her lover inside to introduce him to me. But I said that if he put so much as a foot in the door I would get the poker and brain him. And she knew I would have done it too. The first time I saw her I was hitchhiking. Near Roermond. The rain froze where it fell and the windshield of her car was almost iced over. Otherwise I wouldn't even have stuck out my thumb. One of those beautiful birds in a great big American car. I was studying sculpture in Amsterdam. At the Academy. During the winter holidays students were invited by the municipality of Valkenburg to hack reliefs in the grottos of the St. Pietersberg. Lifesize representations of religious scenes that the mayor and his aldermen hoped would promote tourism. I was working on a Raising of Lazarus. But I had lost interest since messing up the head of Christ. There was a fossilized sea-urchin in it and to get it out whole I had chipped out too much of the marl. A few days later, in the hall of the hotel, the fossil, liberated from the head of the Son of God, fell and pulverized like a ball of brown sugar. That same evening the head waiter quarrelled with me for criticizing the food and dirtying the ceiling. The fodder they put in front of us had really been nauseating. Stew. Great lumps of meat in brown slop. Like shovelling up shit. Artists are greedy and uncritical. They had all started to splash it on their plates, but I suddenly pushed the serving dish away and banged my fist on the table. "This is whale meat," I shouted. Everyone began nipping at it cautiously, as if expecting bones. It was examined, tasted, sniffed. The waiter was called. He couldn't deny a thing, but considered the name "Game pie" quite justified. The whales had been captured and canned for consumption years ago. But you can't force everything down people's throats, so the cans had been dumped on hotels, where it was expected that the hungry tourist would stuff himself silly on the world's largest corpses. No-one in the room had the stomach for another spoonful, and some went to the can to rinse out their mouths, or to puke. The table was cleared and we weren't given anything else to eat. Except for dessert: little pink puddings so tough that, when we rebelled and flung them at the ceiling, they left not a trace on the plaster. The next day I was called in by the manager of the hotel, a pasty-faced man with a tiny chin tucked into the flabs of his neck who should have had a harelip. He said, in that peculiar language they speak down there in Limburg, that I had completely ruined my fellow students' appetite. That the stew, a delectable dish, much valued by distinguished German and Belgian visitors in the summer—when it was paraded on the menu as *Ragoût de Viande et de Légumes*—had landed in the hog tub through my doing. That he was going to enter a complaint with the town council so they'd send me back to Amsterdam. I told him to save himself the trouble as I had planned to leave in a few days anyway, after the Carnival. So I stayed and saw how the entire population of that small Catholic city, not daring to look at another man or woman the rest of the year, went horizontal. If you came into your hotel room without warning you looked straight into an alien cunt, with some drunk hastily wrangling his pipe out of his fly beside your bed. I saw how beer is converted into seed and thence spread about the halls and passages, spurting into the ladies amid the capering and boisterous singing of something I remember as: *Yah, that wench, yah that piece, ich will have her, Yah, that wench, yah that piece, ich will putsch her, She hast me oh, she hast me ah, she hast me folderolderah.* On Ash Wednesday I was off before the male inhabitants of the township, their flies lined with cakes of dried-up white flood but their brows stamped with remission, had come to. In my duffelbag on top of my belongings I stuffed a short fur coat with a beautiful blue sheen that I found in the hall, abandoned like a rag, with a sticky patch to prove that the whack had safely landed in the right pelt. And that's how I came to be standing by the roadside near Roermond. Like I said, it was freezing. My breath hung on me like the speech balloon of a comic strip character. My shoes froze to the ground and my trousers were covered with a layer of ice and crackled when I moved. But all misery was soon forgotten once I had tossed my bag in the boot and huddled beside her in that big thing. The car went all foggy inside as the ice melted and my trouser legs got wet and chilly between the thighs. She had to slow down every so often for big branches lying on the road, broken off the heavy-frosted trees like matchsticks. I watched her legs move elegantly, as if playing the pedals of a Hammond organ. The landscape was being pulled past us on both sides of the car. Smudged peasant hovels among untidy willow groves and ochre rushes. The shits really, if one wasn't sitting beside a beautiful girl, by a

23

shiny dashboard where Cliff Richard was singing "Living Doll". Got the one and only walking, talking, living doll. If you had to go through it like that farmer for instance, on a bike with a scarf around your nut. When the pale sun came through the clouds, the trees shimmered as if they stood in molten glass. And sometimes, at a sharp turn, we seemed to dive straight into it. I kept glancing at her face. Her cheeks, soft and freckled. The beautiful red hair about which I had already asked if it was real and when she said yes I had said something like it being what they called Venetian blonde. I had smiled at her when I sang with Cliff Richard a moment later: "Look at her hair, it's real." In the meantime I wondered if her pubic hair would be as red. I moved a little away from her so that when she looked up I could at least see her eyes without immediately being held captive. Magnificent eyes. The loveliest I had ever seen. They were brown. Golden. I was reminded of what a friend who studied biology once said when he was holding up a plump toad in his hand: "If I ever meet a woman with eyes like these, I'll ask her to marry me then and there." He did follow it up with FUCK! and put the warty beast back in the terrarium after it had pissed in his hand. But something like that wouldn't put me off. Like a cherub pissing on your tongue. And as I was contemplating her face and the freckles, it occurred to me that with this stump of a cigarette casually between my lips I probably looked like a proper thug again. And since she wasn't at all surprised that I was an artist, I culled some incidents from the bohemian life in Amsterdam for her. Nothing too drastic of course. I didn't want to overwhelm her by voicing my rut like a male animal beating his breast, with the filth and slime of the artist's true

24

life. I told her how one time at the Academy I had dunked a blonde nude model in the clay bin and rubbed the greasy grey sludge all over her. She had cooed and bitten, and then spent close to an hour at the washbasin cleaning herself off with old dusters, in every manner of provocative posture. I omitted to add that she did take her revenge. Sweet revenge. When everyone had gone she suddenly pushed me against the wall and proceeded to jack me off and when the seed came she flicked it to the ground with the loose force of her hand and said: "There!" Then she swept out of the classroom swinging her shoulder-bag. And about the time in the anatomy room when we had put two skeletons on top of one another in mating position. When the lecturer entered—we called him Pipe Dream because he smoked a little pipe and treated the skeletons as lovingly as if they were girls—he made out like he had put that creaking fuck session together himself. Not moving a muscle in his own face he went straight into a dissertation on all the muscles that perform the work in such an interaction. And the girls blushed scarlet and everyone got a headache eventually. Because he took three hours. And when he untwined the skeletons and picked them off the ground he tartly huffed the smoke from his little pipe through a ribcage and said: "If you want to know how it works when the woman lies on top, have them ready again next week." She laughed with the corners of her mouth drawn up high and her belly shaking. When we passed a truck on the slippery road and she had to keep both hands on the wheel, I suddenly put my hand on the knees which just escaped the bottom of her skirt. And they weren't of the bony variety with kneecaps sticking out to give you the creeps or those undefined, pale milk puddings either. They

25

were splendid, awe-inspiring samples of plastic art, to quote our art history professor drivelling on about Greek sculpture. I hadn't taken years of anatomy for nothing. She didn't push my hand back when we had passed the truck and didn't clench her thighs when I moved up a little on the inside. Therefore I proposed that we pull over to the side and get on with it. I watched her eyes go misty. So I put my other hand on her neck and softly scratched her where her hair stopped and nipped her little earlobe carefully, like a jackdaw. She shot into the safety zone and before the car had quite stopped we were lying in each other's arms. She slipped down with her thighs parted so I could feel past her panties and give my fingers free play in that moist little slit of hers. From her neck I had gone down in her sweater to stroke her back. When she bent forward with pleasure and I could look into that shady valley between her shoulder blades, I saw it was covered with dark speckles like the back of the seats in the Cinema Royal. With her left hand—fortunately I carry on the left—she was stroking, at first almost by accident but then purposefully the piece of hard-rubber in my still damp jeans. She scraped her nails over the cloth like she was going to tear it to shreds. With the nails of her other hand she clawed furrows in my back. She had pulled the back of my shirt out of my trousers and slipped her hand inside. But how was I to get her from behind the wheel onto my seat? And could I be sure she wanted to get screwed? Cautiously I began to move her a little and without a word she slid smoothly under me, caressing all the while. I just pushed her panties to one side to avoid giving her time to reflect during a complicated manoeuver. She was drugged and weak with desire. When I thrust she said in a trance: "Don't give me a baby, don't give me a baby," and repeated it every time she came and when from my panting she thought that it was on its way. But I kept holding back when I came close by looking very intently at a box on the backseat that had HERMES LTD.—WHOLESALE MERCHANTS OF DOMESTIC UTENSILS on it in vile red letters. When it came anyhow I shot backwards striking my back painfully against that whole shiny collection of controls, cigarette lighter, light this, light that, radio and windscreen washer. She moved back as smoothly as she had slipped down, adjusted something between her legs and drew her skirt snugly to her knees. She only asked, while stretching her mouth before the rear-vision mirror and wiping away some lipstick smudges with a wet finger: "Did anything go in dearest?" Dearest, I thought, dearest, jeezus. She had said it so sincerely. She obviously didn't regard me as just another stud to get laid by. Or maybe she did. Fair enough. But still— dearest? I showed her what was running down the car seat and her eyes went misty again. Coming on a bit like Mack the Knife, I said: "Not a drop, dearest." We both laughed. While I was cleaning up the mess with my handkerchief I asked her if she didn't love me just a little bit. And she said: "A big bit. Or I wouldn't have stopped for you. I never give anybody a ride. Except you." I was so charmed that when I went to zip up my jeans I simply forgot that my prick wasn't tucked into my underpants yet. I gave out a yelp of pain and couldn't move from then on. The skin of my cock was caught in the metal teeth. At first we laughed, since I thought I could work it loose like I used to with the skin of my neck in the zips of jumpers. And I said that right now I could use the inventor of the zipper in that story by Tucholsky. But she had never heard of it. As much as I fiddled

I couldn't open the miserable damned thing. It looked like raw human flesh pinned between the switches of tramrails. My prick stayed upright from the pain, stiff and comical with its red point, and the skin forced between the copper was turning purple. At the least motion I could have screamed in agony. There was nothing else to do but pry the zipper open with some small pliers. But in all of that huge car there was, so help me god, not one pair of pliers. I told Olga to drive somewhere, anywhere, that we had to borrow some pliers. First she thought of a garage. But you can't very well tell them as they go to open up the bonnet that the problem is with the wires indoors. She wiped the steam off the windows and drove away carefully because the least bump made me wail like a woman in labour. She turned into the first side-road and stopped at a small farmhouse. I watched her walk up the doorstep with her lovely bum. Ring the bell. A big woman in an apron answered the door. Olga talked to her. Much too long. What was she bullshitting about? Where the hell were those fucking pliers? I looked through the window, sick with pain. The woman shuffled back into the house. Then a shrivelled mannikin in a faded blue smock came and stood in the doorway. What the hell was going on? Again, talk, talk, talk. No wonder Marx had such little faith in the rural pro-letariat. They have their worth but it takes them a while to see the light. When he finally produced the pliers he wanted to come with her. She managed to restrain him halfway down the steps. Then I had to break that zipper open bit by bit while they peered at us from the farm house across the fuchsias or some bloody vegetable or other. At last I picked those barbed hooks of copper out of my tormented member in a critical bit of fishing that made the water rise around my teeth. Olga looked on with an anguished face, but mostly she couldn't look at all. Then she put her hand softly on my thigh and I cracked something about God's punishment being immediate. When it was done and I carefully laid my prick in my underpants like a wounded Gaul, Olga took the pliers back. The door was opened before she could ring. The eyes vanished from the windows. They must have been worried about the pliers. Before Olga could return, me and my sore limb got gingerly out of the car and fetched the fur coat from the boot. I figured that since I felt half skinned myself, she had certainly earned a little fur. She said it was blue fox. Very costly fur. When she asked how I happened to have it I told her that I had traded it with someone for a rare fossil I had found hacking at the head of Jesus. She didn't ask any more questions, just turned the car around and drove back to the road. We were silent— what could she say. That she was so sorry for my prick? Or, how's your cock doing? Tense. We barely knew each other. But suddenly we started to laugh. At the same time. Louder and louder. I slapped myself on the thighs so hard that the pain froze me in that position. I think it was the laughter that caused the accident. Because she was suddenly on the left hand side of the road with a car coming the other way and she had to jerk the wheel so abruptly that we started to skid. She cried out as if all at once she was floating in the air. The car spun around its axle. I saw the trees along the road swing by as though they'd torn loose. Then the car plunged across the road and crashed straight into a tree. I flew forward. It was like being shot at a terrifying speed into a tunnel of ice. The unremitting beats of the percussion. My mouth was full of sharp hard bits I was sure were my teeth. I spat them out. My face felt lukewarm.

As I stroked it my hand came away red and sticky. I dared not feel my skull for fear I'd be grappling in my brains. Then I looked beside me and saw Olga. I got one hell of a fright. She looked dead. She was lying forward with the steering wheel in her ribs and her tongue hanging out. Her eyes were open. I had the feeling I had been watching her like that for an hour before I began to push the door open. Then I pulled her out. The fur coat clung torn around her body so tightly that I was afraid she couldn't breathe. I took it off and threw it away, lifted her in my arms and stumbled to the road. The blood dripped from my head onto her face, ran down her neck and between her clothes. I just stood there holding her and sobbed, because I thought she was dead. Three cars had passed us. I couldn't wave them down. I held her up and I screamed. Two of the drivers looked straight into my bleeding mug and drove on. None of that mess in my car. And then a little old English car came along. A wartime Morris. It stopped. Out came a slender Englishman who ran up to me with his arms stretched out and said very quietly: "Can I help you, sir?" When I passed Olga over to him he folded at the knees and together they fell to the ground before my feet with her blood-stained face draped over his light raincoat. How he ever managed to get us into the back of that small car of his and to the hospital I'll never know. I was under the impression that Olga stood up by herself, but she couldn't remember it later. Or that she cried out: "The car, oh, that beautiful new car." I do remember that once I was sitting with my arm around her trembling body on that little green-leather backseat. I explored the back of my teeth with my tongue and then looked out at her car. The wreck that had suddenly become our car. The windscreen was white as snow and there

was a bulge with a tiny hole in the middle where I
had struck my head. That must have been where the
sharp, hard bits in my mouth had come from. The
wreck and the ground around it was sown with staves
of ice that had fallen off the tree from the jolt. And
among the glistening litter like a run-over animal lay
the poor rag of a fur coat.

Someday Sweetheart

We had seen the Wondrous Freaks of Nature. The
shin-bone growing together with a tree. The calf
with a harelip. The Mongoloid Calf with a Dog's
Head, born at farmer Herms', Winschoten, on April
3, 1952. Concentration camp whips. Thick with tar-
like blood. The Siamese Calf's Head. Pale muck in
cloudy fluid—it might have been half-rotten pickled
pork in glass jars picked up from a bankrupt village
butcher. But then you discovered a pale eye in it.
Like a button hole in dirty underwear. Arch Enemy
No. 1: CANCER. Step right up and see it! We saw
it and she had the creeps the whole way. Perhaps
because she was thinking of her mother. But I didn't
know about that at the time. About the amputated
breast. The second time I saw Olga she was sitting
at a table by the pancake booth on the Nieuwmarkt
in the shadow of the trees. Less than two months after
the accident. That's probably why we stayed clear
of the bumper cars without a word or a joke. We did

however board a rickety vehicle to take us through the House of Horrors. This time she sat on my right and it was just like we were going through the accident again in a dream. She sat quietly beside me, against me, and didn't scream when hairy threads trailed in our faces or when a light revealed a thick web of rope and threw a bluish reflection on a chalky spider with a body the size of a coconut or when a skeleton lit up in the dark. The only terrors in the pitch-black space were the briefly illuminated pieces of pavement, and white seams that showed you how the whole structure had been thrown together with loose boards that might move in on each other and send you into a chilling pit of death and destruction as in Poe's tale. But when we rode out from this darkness through swinging doors at the end of a set of huge ribs bending over us like arches she screamed. Sharp and piercing. And pressed her face into my sweater. I helped her out of the car and squinting against the bright light we walked away from the fairground through the toffee-apple licking, candy-floss nosing, great plush-bear lugging, rifle-shooting public to the accompani-ment of the blaring music and the screech and rumble of the merry-go-rounds. The moment I saw her sitting at that table there, I felt the glass of the wind-screen in my trap again. I was so glad to see that red, misty creature. And she was delighted to see me because she brushed the hair off my forehead to look at the little scars. I had other scars but she didn't ask about those. Anyway, I could hardly have pulled my cock out to show her that, after eight weeks, those purple zipper wounds were still visible. As if some fiend with a set of square teeth had bitten into it lengthwise. I hadn't been to the Academy for two months. The first few weeks because I ached so much from the accident that I could only stumble around

with a stick and had to wear sunglasses because my
eyes were sore and I saw double. Yet in the hospital in
Eindhoven where they took X-rays and pushed me
on the head so much I thought they wanted to
break my neck, they said that I didn't have con-
cussion. Later I went to Alkmaar a few times a week
hoping to see her. I spent hours in the porchway
across from the family business. I wanted to write
on the round, blue-enamelled door plate with a golden
Hermes complete with helmet, staff and wings on his
ankles: I LOVE YOU! I AM WAITING FOR YOU,
COME TO ME. I CAN NEVER FORGET YOU!
I never saw anybody move behind the windows of
the living quarters over the shop. When I telephoned
the tart voice of an office girl answered: "Hermes
Ltd." Then I quickly put down the receiver without
saying a word. If I waited too long the same voice
said coldly: "Don't bother to phone again. You must
be aware by now that Miss Olga is not available."
If I had known then about the knives from the war
I would have made myself out to be the president of
a camping association looking for sturdy cutlery:
"We don't mind knives made during the war. There
is not the least objection to metal stamped with
GOTT MIT UNS or HEIL HITLER or WIR
HABEN ES NICHT GEWUSST. However, I had
not yet been initiated into the secrets of the business
world. The first time I rang up and asked for Olga
I was put through and got her mother. She had no
intention of calling Olga to the telephone for me.
That we had narrowly escaped death together failed
to impress her. The loss of a brand-new car was bad
enough. She added that if I continued to bother Olga
she would take steps I would not particularly enjoy.
At her honey-sweetest of course, but "My husband
and I do not care to have our daughter involved in

33

friendships of this nature." What did she mean? That I was a budding artist and as such considered unable to earn even dry crusts? Or did she mean, a character that sits in the car beside her daughter with his fly undone. Because that is how they must have heard it from the police who didn't think for one moment that she had had a flat tyre and then lost control of the wheel. They leaned into our youth and how they could understand young people with an arm around each other or having a bit of a cuddle. And they ended by insinuating that one of us, or maybe both, had been putting our hands in the wrong places. I suppose a police dog had tracked down a drop of honest to goodness sperm in the wreck that hung from the tow-truck in the inner courtyard of police head-quarters. And their eyes kept straying suspiciously to my open fly and the white triangle it revealed below my jacket. But they could just as easily have assumed that it had torn in the accident as the legs of my jeans were full of small tears like the bark of a young and growing tree. "A flat tyre was it? You're both sure of that are you?" Then the awkward police report, haltingly read out: "By me, officer-in-charge such and such, drawn up etcetera." The main thing was that I had found her again. And on the way to my studio she said that her parents had gone on holiday to Austria. For three weeks. I thought, then you can live with me for three weeks, but I was afraid to suggest it to her, afraid she would refuse. She suggested it herself. Sitting on the back of my bicycle with her arms around my waist. And as I reflected on the treasure of her well-rounded bottom on the carrier behind my bent back, I put some added care into riding the bicycle. So as not to bump the state of things around. And I resolved not to behave like an animal right away like I had in her car. Because that kind of thing just caused a big mess in the long run. And that's how it was. We sat on the floor in my studio and talked for hours till darkness crept in on us. And we kept playing the only two records I owned. Benny Goodman's second jazz concert: *"Hello, this is Benny Goodman and it seems to me that I have heard that thing before. You may have heard it too, as well as the other numbers..."* We certainly had in the end. At least ten times around with "Someday Sweetheart", "Stardust", "My Gal Sal", "Josephine", "Everybody Loves My Baby", "You Turned the Tables on Me". Meanwhile she talked. First about her father because she loved him most. About his snot-mania. The bullet park under his chair. About his fat body rocking with laughter when she came home all stiff from the accident and couldn't sit because of the pain, about him not being angry about the car at all. And responding to all of her mother's lamentations: "Why worry yourself about a piece of tin, woman." How he would walk to the window if there was a downpour or a storm and say genially: "The weather is bad, just like people." One time she and a girlfriend had planned to join in in chorus at the exact moment because you could count down to when he said it. And they sang out together, she and her girlfriend. But he kept quiet and shook with laughter. Because in some things he had a piglike cunning. The sound of his coughing around the house. Penetrating up to her room where she was lying on the bed reading *Under Mother's Wings* and *Miss Headstrong*. That when she had her thumb in her mouth he carefully drew it out like a cork from a bottle, saying: "Your fingers aren't lollypops, now are they, little doll?" What her mother said when she was around ten and had come in on her in the bathroom and seen the raked flesh where that breast d been taken away: "That's because of the suckinᵍ

35

you did." And for a long time she thought that breasts went away when you had a child, that the baby ate its way through them. About primary school. The first rough boyfriends. The bullies: "I'm going to tie you up!" Pressing her arms cross-wise over her chest, keeping them there with one hand and having a feel with the other. She and her girlfriend had once tied up a boy with a blue-checquered towel. The girlfriend had said to him: "Geronimo is free if he eats a worm." They made him say it after them. "Indian Chief is free if he eats a worm," he said meekly and joyfully with a faraway look in his eyes as if he was taking a shit. They took a worm from underneath a stone in the school playground and laid it on his tongue, which he held out as if receiving the communion wafer. And with his lips drawn back so they could see better he had bitten into the worm and swallowed it. Then he said: "Now I am free." They untied him and he went for a drink of water at the tap. She looked at me earnestly and said: "If you eat a worm you're free. I really believe that. But I could never do it." I took her hands and drew her to her feet and began to dance with her. "I hadn't anyone till you, I never gave my love till you, And through my lonely heart..." I lit a few candles because it was the era when artists celebrated with sour *vin ordinaire* by candlelight. The candles stuck in the empty bottles. I was reminded of what I'd heard someone say once at a party: "It's the round plump ones that swing around that are the best." So I lifted her skirt and pulled her panties down her bottom and when she had her back to the mirror I danced on the spot and watched those magnificent cheeks swing to and fro. Shameless in the candlelight. I felt so bloody rich. But then she looked over her shoulder and exclaimed, surprised and half-indignant: "You're looking at

36

me!" She wanted me to let her go so she could pull her panties up and her skirt down. But when I quickly turned so she could see me moving against that naked piece of hers, she left it. I could feel the warmth of her body through my trousers and I knelt down before her and kissed her belly, her thighs, and then I had that juicy cunt of hers between my lips. And it wasn't one of those things with odd clumps of hair around it which made you feel like you're kissing a man with a beard or the sort of equipment that has the lips hanging out, great brown flippers like the swinging-doors in a saloon, all set and ready to knock you in the balls. No, even though I had only glanced at her little tuft I had seen enough. The way her occasionally freckled belly slipped down like a brown bean between the gleaming wheat of the *Song of Songs,* ebbed briefly below and then swelled again with the firmness of a young girl's small breast. A ripe, red-haired, rosy fruit with a notch that stood open with milky sap. I gripped her backside with both hands, pulled her to me and stuck my tongue into that juicy notch. She groaned and grunted and her high heels ticked the ground with trembling tension and she convulsed forward and her hands on the top of my head pressed my face into that soft profusion of flesh. Turning her cunt around my tongue. Then she pushed me away from her but my chin got stuck behind the elastic of the panties tensed around her legs so I got in one last little lick. I recalled what I had read in a French translation of the Kama Sutra: *Exitées directement par la succion, l'aspiration et le lèchement de tous leurs organes, les femmes, parvenues au paroxysme, lancent dans la bouche de l'homme, par leur conduit afférent, le mucus glaireux sécrété par les glandes vulvo-vaginales.* I had always thought this an exaggeration and that Henry the Fourth who was so mad for it he would

have eaten it off a plate—my kingdom for a cunt—
had been the victim of his overheated imagination.
He liked it better than oysters. I don't like oysters
but now that it had landed on my tongue I had to
admit, while watching Olga sway, eyes half-closed
in the aftermath of pleasure, that it was very tasty.
All of a sudden Olga pressed her hands to her pussy and
said that she was bursting to go. I said she was welcome to piss in my mouth. She called me a pig and ran
to where I'd shown her, the basin at the other end
of my studio. And when she, a bit shy but nonetheless
putting her backside fair and square over the job,
was pissing half-hidden behind a potted fig, I was
glad that she hadn't accepted my proposal. Because
there was such a pelting that it sounded like a goat
splashing away on galvanized iron. I was so hot for
her that I ran up before she could finish and forced
my hand down between her legs to hold it in that
lovely warm urine. Then I rubbed it around my
face. She made a dirty face but I said that nothing
smells so delicious as the piss of a healthy young
woman. Provided she's not a beer drinker. Very
healing too. On stinging-nettle burns for instance.
After that I picked her and her wet cunt up and
carried her to my bed kissing and licking her face.
Including her ears and her nostrils. Bitter and salty.
When I had undressed her, which she willingly
allowed, stretching lazily, I put all the candles on
boxes and benches around the bed. Then I sat down
on a chair to behold her at my ease. The breasts
that didn't fall away like soft puddings but stayed
firmly upright with the nipple to the ceiling. And her
nipples, not those brown marbles that look as if you
could flick them off with your fingers, but truly the
rosy extremities of magnificently domed temples.
They were specked with hundreds of tiny freckles

as if strewn with brown sugar. And her skin was so white and fair between all those brown flecks that it seemed she must always wash with buttermilk soap. Her sweet, round face and the chestnut hair waving over the pillow and those great, dark eyes quietly looking around. At my studio. At the plants, the nude studies, at the bed with the candles around it reflected in the mirror. I left to go to the lavatory and when I came back she had fallen asleep with one small hand to her red pussy and the other against her cheek. I sat down on the chair again and watched her. Then I saw that her lips had parted and that her thumb had gone inside and that she was slowly sucking it. How long I sat there fascinated by that lovely creature I don't know. I saw the candles die one by one. Some of them hissing when the last bit of wax sagged down through the neck of the bottle with the burning wick and fell in the dregs. I heard the birds begin singing like madmen and the pigeons coo and mutter long before light came and the cold of the morning woke her. I crept in with her, spread the sheet lightly over us, and our night began.

The Apple of Revenge

When these American creatures with their parakeets and their art books (That pisspot Dürer and his frizzy hair) and their clutch of boyfriends had fled the scene—I recall they had underpants made

39

of some kind of elastic weave that pressed the whole business together—I was back at my old tricks again. Well, not quite the same old tricks. A chastening, you might say, from loneliness and suffering. And from longing for my redhead. In any case I stopped wielding my prick like a harpoon ready to poke the first blubber that rose over the waves of Amsterdam-by-night. Instead I looked for what is known as soul. I picked up girls who were visibly distressed. Girls you could talk with before the lollypop was produced. About death, misery, illness, inverted nipples—incurable, you can suck at them as passionately as you like until they pop out like fiery buds; the saliva is hardly cold and then flop, they sink back into the porous fabric of those milk-mops—about home, parents, younger sisters, older brother, incest, buggery and pimples. This road was often paved with disaster. To bed a child, as they say, is to get up riled. Well the same applied to my wayside blossoms. Elly, for instance, whom I ferreted out of a telephone booth. I found out too late that she had run away from an institution. I thought she was just fat and foolish and a pathological liar until we were in bed that evening and she told me how she had cut the canvas out of a highchair because her little sister had shitted on it and now she had poked out the eyes of all the people in the paintings at home. When I woke up in the morning she was sitting bolt upright beside me in bed with a strange staring look in her eyes and her arms fiery and raw. When I asked her what the bejesus she was up to, she said: "I fancied a bit of skin." To top it off she had wet the bed and me. Then there was Eveline, a Protestant, a dark, long-haired, spindly little wretch with breastlets as limp as a collection pouch and one of those tight little anchovy cunts. I spent all night sweating and pounding in an effort to make her forget the 1886 Dissension. And then, so help me, she had the gall to say the next morning, with a tight-lipped mouth: "I missed God between us." Shows you the uses a trio can be put to. And you wouldn't want to joke about fucking better than God and so on because that gave her a fit and she would talk your early-morning full-bladder erection down by reciting the articles of faith. And Truus, a Catholic, fat from gorging on fish every Friday and french-kissing with a mouth as full of water as the holy font. When I'd heard all her troubles and wanted to start screwing her, it turned out she was having her period. She did say when she went to the toilet that she had the sickness of the great pain, but how was I to know? I imagined she had the shits. And I didn't notice it when we were playing around because she used "Invisible Protection", so that my prick incautiously got stuck in the dryness. When I wanted to stick it in higher up she said: "That's not what a mouth is for." It wouldn't have done any good to suggest that this was merely the sacred host, because she would only have tied my cock in a knot. But it was still preferable to being called Old Otter, Quince, or Hairy Pudding, or whatever they'd heard their parents blather to one another in the stale round of twenty-five years of marriage. Or when they had the Passionate Mediterranean Lover complex like that mean peroxide Bertie who said as she greedily watched me go when I unwound myself from her long enough to go to the can: "You walk just like an Italian fisherman." Then you really had to look out. Oh, *mamma mia*. Inside of a few days I had a letter from her guardian whom she had recruited as match-maker: "In connection with your association with Bertie, whose guardian I am, I would appreciate a visit from you." Like falling into *Vanity Fair*. And seven months later she could be seen in the Kalverstraat lumbering behind a pram with a dark-haired, brown-eyed baby, clearly made on the twilit shore between Genoa and Naples by an Italian fisherman with the blood and scales of tuna in his pubic hair, sand chafing her damp butt and the noise of voices and song drifting over the water, as if the sea was the gallery of an opera house during the interval. The little Surinam half-caste who danced in the chorus of an African ballet group and was very upset because those jet-black leapers looked on her as only half-baked: "You are nothing at all. Coffee with milk. *Du café et du lait.*" Who responded to everything I had to say with: "Poop off, go tell it on the toilet." Who made funny faces at me and crinkled her sweet little nose and called me Peter Rabbit and who kissed me when I twisted my own face for her and said: "Let me give the little beastie a kissie." Pale Willy who had looked too long into the coffee-grounds and came to visit me at the studio with a pram full of dear and peaceful negro baby lying amongst the shopping under a white parasol with little flowers. And who with the help of the cashier's slip calculated exactly how much I owed her for the time my cat expertly unwrapped a package of steak while we were fooling around and ate it up between the kicking legs of her dark baby. Anne, who said that she hated all men because her father used to pick her up saying he was going to tickle her and then ran his rough, unshaven cheek against hers, and laughed uproariously when she fled, tears in her eyes. She didn't want to fuck, turned her shanks on me and told me that to her "Goddammit" was prussian-blue (she had taken an arts course). In the middle of the night when I took her after a sleep-drugged fight of legs she couldn't come.

No matter how tender I was or what I tried with her she stayed an empty tyre that wouldn't be pumped up. The girl with the boxer who fell for me so desperately that she wanted to save herself for the wedding night. When that fell through she walked by my house every day with her face turned away, pining. When her dog lifted his leg against the tree across the street she'd glance up at the windows. But if, hindlegs trembling, he decided to press out a turd that rooted him to the ground, she impatiently drew him on. Then I could see the shame creep into her neck as if it had been her squatting there taking a shit. For my birthday she put a large mussel shell by the door of my studio. She had lined the mother-of-pearl with moss and put in red berries and imitation pearls and other crap. Beside it was a card with a Picasso reproduction of a girl with a flat face like her and large melancholy eyes. Unlike her own, unfortunately. On the back she had written: *How lonely you must be, if you no longer feel it. How quiet you must be and longing doesn't speak.* But suddenly I'd had enough of it again. I put a stop to it. I didn't feel like it any more. The very sight of a skirt made me puke. At first I thought I might be impotent from sleeping with a girl who had so much hair on her chest that it was like lying between coconuts. But that wasn't it. I simply couldn't find it. Find her. Olga. In all those broads that the winds had swept haphazardly into my bed I found only a small piece of what I desired so strongly, what I longed for like a madman. One girl might have her eyes (not quite, or it would have been enough), another her behind, her voice, her navel, her hips, or was covered with freckles like the asphalt of Fifth Avenue after a ticker tape parade like my red darling. But even if I had set up a harem with all those Olga-like bits and

43

pieces I could not have constructed her whole person out of the jigsaw. The worst was yet to come. I began to talk about it. About her and about my own misery. What she looked like. Her hair, her eyes and, as I became more confidential, her cunt, her bum, her tits. How she was. That she had said once as she was washing the windows: "Have you noticed that window sills have a special smell?" And when I asked her what they smelled of, she said: "Wet window." And the time shortly after she came to live with me that I asked her if she wanted to come to *The Cherry Orchard*. And she replied with relish and greed in her voice: "Yes, where is it?" When I told her it was a play by Chekhov she had been a bit embarrassed and said she knew that and just wanted to know the name of the theatre. I'm sure she thought it was an orchard where you could eat as many cherries as you liked for a few guilders. A few days later I brought her a big bag of cherries. She blushed, but once she got stuck into them she said: "That must be the worst thing about being dead. Never to eat cherries again." The morning we slept in and heard a shrill old woman's voice underneath our window calling "Yoohoo, yoohoo, yoohoo—Fritz!" when she said: "How terrible to be Fritz." And about the bumble bee, I told that one a few times too. "How nice to be a bumble bee. A cosy fat body in a striped woollen jumper between a couple of little gauze wings." When I said it my eyes swelled with tears and I had to be careful not to blink or they would run down (she had owned such a jumper with stripes but I burnt it when she left). But before it got to crying the tawny arms of some compassionate, fading wallflower were wrapped around my shoulders. Because they have an instinct for gauging the watermark of eyes. And then they plunge in like a butterfly at the nectar-filled

44

flower cup. I should like to write: "We now observe the hero of this tale in the stage of mental crisis, caught in the despair of isolation and introspection, listing heavily against a comforting bosom." If only I could write so ironically. About myself as a hero. Then I would no longer be the victim of this story and it would be me pulling the strings. But I can't raise any bloody hero. I see myself in a pathetic state. Crocodile tears and all. I see myself at a party, in a corner, pressed against an older woman. But not so that you'd say, "Look, they're at it"; it would be more a case of long-lost son. She has thrown comforting arms around me while behind us the mad party surges on frantically with "Rock Around The Clock" and "Yes Tonight Josephine" between broken glass and cigarette butts. Hell, I confess, I'm crying now. You can tell from my shoulders. That I'm trying to hold back. Breaking down on a woman I don't know from a hole in the ground. She must be strange in any case, otherwise she'd be rocking now or twisting about on bare feet, dancing lasciviously. She has buck teeth that press into her lower lip as she talks. At parties I came to be known as the quiet boy with the marble-white prematurely-sunken cheeks. Sometimes I overheard someone remark: "It was that redhead, eh?" or "You don't see much of that these days. Usually they're glad when they bugger off." And the coarser types: "Why should he give it a second thought? They're all the same when you're on them. Cunt is cunt said the farmer as he screwed his own pig." But these consoling, motherly women did teach me something. Because some of them had daughters the same age as Olga. And one imperious shrew told me when I was talking about my one-titted mother-in-law and asked how a mother could deliberately plunge her

45

daughter into such a mess: "Every mother is a stepmother for her daughters." And it gave me a jolt as I remembered Olga saying how the beginning of *Snow White* had made a tremendous impression on her as a child. Her mother, who thought it was too horrible, hadn't wanted to read her the story, but her father had. Of the queen who looked at the snow through a window set in an ebony frame. Pricking her finger with a needle and saying while she looked at the blood: "Would that I had a child as white as snow, as red as blood, and as black as this ebony." Black, white and red. The colours stayed in her mind as the story's terror. Then I knew that her mother, though she didn't know it consciously, hadn't wanted her to read it because the story was the mirror that not only told her who was the most beautiful but also showed her the poisoned apple she had already prepared for her step-daughter. I see that foul bitch in the guise of an old woman and my hate almost made me write that she didn't need the disguise. I see her take the apple from her bosom. And then I see it is the cancerous breast, rotten and full of poison, she is thrusting at the lips of my darling. And finally I know that it was always too late. I realize that the piece of poisoned apple will never fall from her mouth, that she will never sit up and ask: "Where am I?" And that I shall never be the prince who vill say: "You are with me. I love you more than ything in the world."

Requiem for a Dead Sparrow

The studio I lived in then had been the home of a resistance fighter who was shot by the Germans. After the war a bronze plaque was attached to the house that read: DIED FOR HIS COUNTRY. Underneath, on a rusty nail that seemed an invitation to hang yourself, a floral tribute was placed in an annual ceremony. A clump of damp peat moss studded with red and white carnations and blue irises. I don't know why but I hated those flowers. Every year I pulled them down before they had wilted and threw them in the dustbin. On a windy day the ribbon with ARTISTS' RESISTANCE 1942–1945 would flutter wildly in front of the window. After Olga went off with that runt it startled me each time I came into the kitchen and caught the movement of the silk streamer out of the corner of my eye. Shock and joy stabbed through me at the thought that she had come back to me in a dress with lots of ribbons and frills, the kind she had begun to wear after she left. That she was at the door, hesitating to ring the bell. When she had been living with me just a short while—right after the trouble with her parents: her father who missed her very much, and her mother who deep down was glad she was out of the way but from cold fury couldn't let it be and had the company car drive her up to our door where she rang and rang the bell for half an hour, stamping her feet like a crazy hen—the children in the neighbourhood had found a dead sparrow, on the fourth of May. They buried him in the flowerbed right under our window. On his back with the head sticking out so he wouldn't get sand in his eyes. A little later on a woman came along to put a bunch of daffodils on the sand before the official memorial service began. Right by the burial mound of the sparrow. I laughed like a drain, but Olga took it into her silly head to go outside and squat by the little head sticking out of the sand because she was afraid he might still be alive. I called her in for I knew this was asking for trouble. And sure enough she began to talk about her dead relatives. Her aunt Sofie who had a heart attack on their stairs and then bumped down on her stomach like a sand bag. Another aunt who'd slowly melted away with cancer. The rolls of rotten meat that stayed in the washcloth when they sponged her. Her grandfather who died at their house when she was twelve. They hadn't been able to close his eyes. He kept leering through the slits. Probably fearing that Hermes Ltd. was in for quick doom under the leadership of his fat kindly son. So she began to cry because the sparrow's dull-shining eyes were standing ajar too. Because she had been her grandfather's pet and he always gave her presents. She sobbed on hysterically and I told her to stop. But she couldn't. She held up her face and said that I would have to hit her. That would cure it. She said it was something from when she was a child. That I couldn't be expected to understand. Without hesitation I hit her hard across her wet cheeks. Hard. When she still didn't stop I threw her on the bed, tugged up her skirt, pulled down her panties, and hit her as hard as I could on the behind with my flat hand. Till her skin was red and swollen and that posterior looked positively delectable. As if she had sat with her arse in stinging nettles. Then I screwed her with my hands under her red-hot behind. Her damp face with trails of red hair clinging to it against my cheek. Her short weepy breath panting in my ear. She came with such full

48

animal cries that I thought they must have heard it outside, right through the solemn ceremony voice. When we got up and walked to the window with drools of seed at cunt and prick and looked at the groups of people who'd stayed behind to chew the fat, she said that the whole time her mind had been on the skates with the brown boots her grandfather had given her as a birthday present soon before he died and that even on the day of his funeral she'd gone skating. That's why she'd had the feeling she was sailing with graceful curves through that cold winter's day when the old man was buried. That it had helped her to forget the funeral voice outside. And she said I was to put the sparrow under the earth or it would stay on her mind. But before I could get down to it the cat had dragged the bird into the kitchen. I picked the thing up with a piece of newspaper, twisted it up and put the parcel in the dustbin. I didn't mention it to Olga and she didn't ask. She was probably done with the whole episode a couple of days later, together with the flowers I told her to take down and put in the dustbin. It sank down in her memory with the skates and little boots which she hung on the wall of her room when they got too small surrounded by old newspaper photos of Sonja Henie, things she wanted to keep forever. When she came to live with me for good her mother phoned the Salvation Army and had them take away the skates and almost all her toys and little girl's books. Her dolls she got rid of herself when she was still young enough to play with them. Weeping and shaking, as they meant a lot to her. But it had to be done. She couldn't stand the sight of them any longer. Once she had been given a very large doll. Nearly as big as a real baby. It could even say "Mama" and open and close its eyes with their lovely long eyelashes.

49

Every day she would take its clothes off and bathe it.
And in the morning before going to school she stuffed
pieces of bread in its little open mouth. After a while
she thought the doll must be sick since it no longer
said "Mama" even though she held it up and down and
sideways. One day as she bent over the cradle
the little face was covered with maggots coming
out of the mouth with quivering, searching feelers.
She wanted to scream but couldn't. She put her
fingertips in her wide-open mouth, bit them, and
froze, watching, until her mother came to say she
would be late for school. She was dragged away
from the cradle crying. When she came home her
father had poured bleach into the doll. The mouth
had lost its colour and the face was streaked.
He had tried to pick out the repulsive dough with a
bent hairpin, but the doll made a squashy sound
when it was moved and halfway through he'd had
enough. She didn't want it any more, or her other
dolls. And she didn't want to give them to her girlfriends either. They had to go. Under the ground.
So her father (her mother had just wanted to throw
them in the dustbin), took his fat stomach amiably
into the garden, rolled up his sleeves, dug a hole and
buried them. Olga told me all this much later and
that's why I wondered if she referred to the business
with the dolls when she said: "It's something from
when I was a child. I can't expect you to understand."
For she had her secrets and took her own time in
revealing them. She'd been with me for two years
before I discovered that her upper front teeth were
false. She had beautiful strong teeth. White and
animal. She took care of them with sickly regularity.
Immediately after meals she picked the bits of food
out with a sharpened goose feather for a tooth pick.
Next she'd brush her teeth extensively, her mouth

50

full of foam. One time when she was again fussing with her teeth, picking them clean by the mirror, she suddenly screamed. With a twisted face and open mouth she ran for her handbag, took out the pocket mirror and angled it in her mouth before the big mirror. Her eyes wide with fear she inspected the back of her teeth. When I asked her what was wrong, she pointed with horror at the toothpick fallen on the floor. I picked it up and saw a maggot on it. I said that bits of food had obviously been left in the quill and a fly had laid his eggs in it. But she wouldn't be reassured. She believed she'd picked the maggot from between her teeth. And then came the story of the crowns. She'd always felt they might come off at any time. For if the roots were bad she wouldn't know about it since the nerves had been killed. She had fallen off an iron gate in the park when she was thirteen. Right on her mouth. Her two upper teeth broke but she'd kept them that way for quite a few years. A boy in the class had said it looked just like an electric socket and as her red hair was even brighter then they called her Redlights at school. I had to laugh and pulled her to me tenderly. But she pushed me away and walked gravely to the telephone and made an appointment with the dentist.

The Lucky Dip Machine

When I see wild ducks in the sky I always remember her saying they were like flying chianti bottles. She

wouldn't shell peanuts since they reminded her of
old men's toes. One time when we went to Ijmuiden
and I asked her if she'd been there before, she said:
"Yes, once. With a bottle of cough syrup." We walked
on the pier arm in arm and watched a tugboat bring
in a gigantic steamer. She stayed by a fisherman
for a long time looking into the creel net where a
bleeding eel was wriggling around while I moved on
because it gave me a pain in my cock. We spent
some time sitting in a sidewalk cafe there in the
sun and watched the flies screwing. It was absolutely
impossible to see how they went about it. She said
that if you had a good look at how they washed
themselves you could never ever kill another fly.
In the shopping arcade leading to the beach, with
wooden stalls and eating shacks like the street sets
in a cowboy picture after the shooting, where it
smelled of fried chips, fruit and fish, and the boys
whistled at her as we passed or said: "What a piece
of arse!" and laughed, whispering filthy things about
her, I let her throw a quarter into the lucky dip
machine. It emitted a dirty white ball like a reptile's
egg. In it was a flesh-coloured blubbery salamander
with a wobbling head and large sad black eyes. It
gave her the creeps and I said it would be fitting
if we sneaked it onto the end of a fisherman's line.
But she wanted to get rid of it then and there and
twisted a hole in the sand with her heel and dropped
it in. Then she shuffled sand over it and pressed down
with her foot. Then there was the time in the Amsterdam Wood among the pines, milky resin running
out of their trunks as blue in the shade as the ground
ivy we were lying in. A rider on a red-brown horse
came by and smiled at us, saying: "My chestnut
for yours?" That was where she told me how she and
a girlfriend had once been caught trespassing in the

dunes around Egmond-aan-Zee by a mounted policeman. He had pulled out his notebook to take down their names when his horse began to piss like a hose from an enormously long and limp pale penis. He tucked the book away quickly and said they'd better get out of there fast. He must have felt that it was his own cock dangling out of his trousers taking a leak in front of those two little girls. Our first few months we spent driving all over The Netherlands. From Ameland to Limburg—avoiding the Pietersberg and the whale-munching tourists—from the lighthouse at Westkapelle to Denekamp. These were also the last months of my student years and I didn't feel like going to the Academy anymore. Art was no match for her. I would start working again some day but first I had to play out my mad infatuation. When her parents returned from their holidays they found a letter from Olga and she didn't mince her words. Not so much severing the tie with her parents, that invisible navel cord, as exploding it. Placenta and all. To keep the record straight I must add that I dictated it. But the fragments hit us in the face later on in the form of underhanded tittle tattle and volleys of hypocrisy. But this didn't affect her father. She was even allowed the car for a while to celebrate our pre-honeymoon weeks. Since they now lived over the office, to economize, he hardly needed the car any more. Just for status. And what better advertisement than to have his beautiful daughter driving about with HERMES LTD.—WHOLESALE MERCHANTS OF DOMESTIC UTENSILS in refined gold lettering on the doors. Right after the accident, when she was afraid to drive, he had pushed her into the new Fiat and told her to get on with it. He didn't need the car for his wife. During the first lesson he gave her she had driven like a headless chicken through a hedge and into someone's garden. Aside from the car she damaged three glasses of orange squash and two of grenadine that were on the garden table when she bumped to a halt against it. And so we landed in Coevorden—where Olga had always wanted to go because the name had stuck from geography lessons. A drag of a place. A village street with a few houses behind it. Not worth the effort she had put into droning off place names in those schoolroom drills. Next thing you knew you were back in the brown crap, the peatlands along the border with Germany where a decent fuck was impossible. You'd probably sink into a pool of boggy blubber, puffing and blowing as you went. And in East Flevoland you were tormented by grey tornadoes of mosquitoes; you took the chance that your limb would be mistaken for a grass snake by the hawks, skimming the marsh in a low glide, or that your eyes would be almost gouged out by a godwit when you left the church before the hymns and your offering shot into his nest and trickled down among the neatly camouflaged eggs. No, doing it in nature's lap was for the birds. It seemed as if all the creatures of the field were in league to prevent us from multiplication. You'd just have your pants down to your knees and be moving in a nice rhythm over the hot moan sighing through her lovely lips and a grub or some other small crawler would try to get into your arse, or, just before the final thrust, Olga would spring up because a yellow-fringed water beetle wanted to take this opportunity to slip inside. Or a grasshopper would come to sit on the end of her nose and her blowing would break into my cadenza. No, fucking was never so good as at home in bed or when we towed the mattress up to the big mirror when we

54

wanted to watch. My balls bouncing against her tail at each lunge, the map of tiny purple veins set between the freckles on her beautiful full back or, if it was her looking into the mirror, her profile as she watched my hairy body ploughing among her soft flesh. Those clouded eyes of hers and hot trembling lips translated into words that throbbed in your head even though she would never pronounce them: "Piss your stuff in me, gorilla. Go on! Come!" But, in that immeasurable polder among yellow colza fields by an asphalt road that shone like water in the heat and ran from one senseless green horizon to the other, we ate smoked eel bought off a fishing boat in Kampen. She couldn't skin them so I had to drop morsels of the soft meat in her mouth like feeding a baby bird. We didn't come across a soul, not even after whistling past the WELCOME TO LELYSTAD AND OUR CHURCH sign on that tacky, smelly tar road. It seemed as though all the inhabitants of those little new houses and barracks had been wiped out by insecticides. A dry and dusty DDT peace reigned. I didn't even spot the familiar dark brown crumpled-up Mars bar wrapper that always looks like a small animal. *Not a breath of wild air.* As we drove back across the Knardijk to Harderwijk into the orange sunset she nestled beside me all sunburnt and rosy with a bunch of camomiles and poppies melting against her body from the heat. At home we took a shower together and I washed the grass seeds out of her cunt hair. We walked around the studio in the nude so I found myself kneeling beside her, kissing her rump and her arsehole that tasted of soap. I stuck a poppy in it and she ran around the studio wriggling her hindquarters because it tickled. But she was quite taken with the idea as she left it in and looked in the mirror every time she went by. I went

55

after her with a ruler till she surrendered and dived onto the bed with her bum in the air and I slapped the flower to red juice and fell asleep over her with my finger in her little cunt because she was in the danger zone. In the middle of the night the cold woke me up and I found my prick in her arse. She had pinned herself on me and was feverishly coming to a climax by putting her fingers through mine into her cunt and blissfully fingering herself. Life was like that in the beginning. At least when it was warm and we had poppies in the house. But in that time something I'm very ashamed of happened. After a while I got a rash on my acorn. I was furious because I thought she had endowed me with clap. She gave her oath, in tears, that long before she met me she hadn't been to bed with anyone. But I didn't believe her and dragged her with me to a skin specialist who said the inflamed knob came from excessive sexual intercourse. When we arrived back home she was furious. I had already registered her angry feet walking home beside me and I didn't quite know what to say. So I quickly put on one of her favourite records. The Phil Woods Jazz Quintet with Jon Eardley. "Pot Pie" and "Mad About The Boy." Well, she wasn't very mad about me just then as she knocked the arm of the gramophone off the turntable, grabbed the record and sailed it through the open window. That must have cooled her down because she suddenly began to laugh uproariously. We were married not long after. For free. Just the fifty cents for the wedding certificate. We went the same way I had first brought her home from the fair. By bicycle. She on the carrier, on which I had laid a soft cloth for the occasion. After all, on the greatest day of her life she shouldn't have to dent her arse. She wore a purple dress and a straw bowler that she had made herself from a Mexican sombrero by cutting off the broad brim. The purple dress I had bought for her from the advance on my first commission. With my first self-earned money. I still had to make a statue for it expressing Motherhood for some park or other but I could worry about that later. At the city hall they ground us through the mill six couples at a time, most of the brides in an advanced stage of pregnancy. One marriage even had to be postponed because labour began in the waiting room. The registrar, however, still troubled to take the time for a short personal speech. He spoke of the blooming love of youth while licking his chops at the sight of my deeply happy darling whose obscene body was squeezed into that purple velvety dress like an eel in its skin. Later, when she had left me and was going through one brief marriage after the other the public servant would cough as he read off the names of previous husbands. We wanted to spend that day lying in each other's arms with a bottle of champagne by the bed, get up when it was dark and eat in the city. But goddammit if the phone didn't get us out of bed every five minutes with one of her or her parents' friends on the other end of the line. It appeared that her mother had announcements printed after all and had spread them liberally over the upper regions of Noord-Holland. Satin-finish paper with little roses embossed on it and our names in gold letters. I resolved to make it clear once and for all to this brand new mother-in-law of mine when we saw them in a few days time to celebrate the wedding that she was to mind her own business. When her father came to collect us I had to sit where Olga used to be, beside him. He called it the dead man's seat, because his doctor had advised him never to go behind the wheel of a car again, he casually told me, his fat foot on the pedal, flying along heedlessly doing a hundred. And then he cracked his first joke. Not the one about the two boys who came for supper, not yet. About two other boys who had met a beautiful girl they were taking to dinner and had arranged that if one of them had the guts to come out with three dirty comments over dinner the other friend would leave him the field. And sure enough, when the Manhattans were brought and she put her cherry aside he asked: "May I have your cherry?" And when the turkey came he served her, saying: "Do you like stuffing?" I knew pretty well what was next, as they came to the end of the turkey: "Shall I save my bone for your pussy?" but I let him finish at his ease and then laughed heartily. And I topped it with one that was perhaps not quite suitable for a newly married man to tell his father-in-law but the man was so endearing and so sweet that I jumped right in like one of the boys. About the skipper and his daughter and his mate who have only one bunk for the three of them to sleep in. The skipper in the middle. When the skipper is well away and snoring noisily the mate half rises, nudges the daughter and says: "Shall we?" She tells him to pull a hair out of her father's baggage first. He thinks this a somewhat strange request, but OK, he is an obliging fellow and one good turn deserves another. This goes on for a few nights and then one morning the daughter and the mate are standing in the bow and the daughter begins to sing: "Last night I had a jolly good time! Yo Ho!" And the mate sings: "Tonight it'll be even more divine! Yo Ho!" And then the deep bass of the skipper suddenly comes out of the wheelhouse: "And if you take, oh take, this line, there'll be not a hair on these balls of mine! Yo Ho, Yo Ho, Yo Ho! Yo Ho, Yo Ho, Yo Ho!" He went into such a con-

58

vulsion that he, like his daughter not so long before
him, shot onto the wrong side of the road. What with
the car coming at us turning on headlights and everyone slamming on their brakes, a disaster was averted.
And while the angry hooting of the other car passed
into the distance he said imperturbably: "That's
how it is in traffic, it all fits exactly. And if it doesn't
fit you hear a bang." No matter. We had escaped
the jaws of death and a moment later we were standing
in the garden amid notables and business associates.
Her mother would rather have had the reception in a
restaurant with a cold buffet finale, but he had dis-
missed every one of the restaurants she named with:
"I know what their food will be like on the 17th of
April 1992." Out of sheer snobbism she had thrown
herself on a novelty that had just blown in from
America, because she was set on having her party.
The Barbecue. With sets of relish in various shades
of puke. So everyone walked about the garden with
eyes full of tears from the smoke and the stench (she
didn't know how to manage the charcoal and had
lit it by pouring on paraffin oil) and holding a lump
of meat that looked like a half-rotted rubber sole
on one side while on the other the blood mingled
with the purple ink of the inspection stamp. Her
father watched it all from his easy chair on the steps,
this time not picking his nose and turning bullets.
He said to me, with good-natured mockery written
on his face: "Let them muck about and chew, It
makes great sport, the barbecue." The tough, burnt
lumps that made people look like chimney-sweeps
around the mouth were pushed out of sight with a
quick, furtive sweep into the petunias and lavender
of the borders, where a German shepherd dog be-
longing to one of the guests dispatched them, growl-
ling. The ninety-ninth toast was proposed by some

59

great-aunt from Haarlem whose bulk was contained in a tent of a dress of some *art nouveau* design which flapped in the wind and wafted a smell of what must have been forty year's worth of camphor towards us. She took it upon herself to offer us her predictions of a happy future in a creaking voice accompanied by her loose dentures. While she was talking, the completely stuffed brute of a dog made his way to the lawn past a tangle of rather embarrassed but dutiful listeners, put his nose to the ground and proceeded to puke with massive jerks of his body. And there, unmistakably, on the grass before everyone's eyes in a sauce of grey gut soup, were seven or eight of those black shoe-soles. Her father was very sweet; he raised himself from his chair, took the napkin from around his neck that she had authoritatively tied on him when she came to press one of those scorched things in his hand, and put it clumsily over the pile of dregs and slime. A ripple of applause accompanied him as he shyly made his way back to his chair. My fear that a latecomer might pick up the napkin thinking that someone had dropped it there fortunately proved to be unfounded. And so a reception that refused to blossom into a merry party faded on the image of the great-aunt from Haarlem running through the bushes with a wasp after her, and that of a lumbering uncle who landed a size fifteen footstep on a glass of sherry that had been left on the grass for a moment and interred it permanently in the lawn. When all the guests had disappeared and the lonely barbecue was sending up its dying farewell, Olga came to get me out of the garden. She said her father wanted to talk to us about money, but that her mother was behind it of course. The scheming bitch. I felt like dumping her and her silk-shrouded rear on top of the barbecue. Olga gave

60

me her hand and we quietly sat down in the sitting room to await events. Then the door opened rather suddenly and she pushed him inside. "Go ahead," she said and steered him into his chair. He draped himself lazily, looked at the ceiling, looked outside, drummed on the side of his chair. The "Radetzky March" I thought. And she tried to compel him to look at her. She gave a ladylike cough and then said with irritated impatience: "Come now, daddy." But he stayed silent, his face getting redder all the time, twisting his head in every direction except ours. She stamped her feet and with a last cantankerous glance at him the words began to spurt out of her. That it had cost them bags of money to make this an unforgettable day for us. That we had pretty well forced them to give permission for the marriage by threatening with a court case but that we mustn't be under the illusion we'd ever get a penny. And that she, Olga, needn't think she could come back in a few months with her tail between her legs. That she had warned her quite explicitly to stay away from artists and their like, people whose life was a chain of poverty and especially hard when you came from a well-to-do, respectable family. And other hysterical and inane platitudes. When she stopped momentarily for a deep breath to propel the poison with greater force, he suddenly said, like a dense fat boy who may not have understood it all but thinks all's well and that an amicable arrangement has been made: "Well, that's agreed then." She sprang up as if she had indeed been sitting on the barbecue and luckily she could unleash her rage on the caterpillar of ash that had fallen on the carpet between my feet. She ran to the kitchen and was back seconds later with a carpet sweeper, rolling it furiously back and forth, bouncing against my shoes. He walked to the sideboard rubbing his hands and quite unperturbed poured himself a glass of Beerenburger, his favourite gin. Then he walked the brimful glass back to his chair without spilling a drop, and as he sucked a margin around the glass he said, with a scarcely concealed sarcasm in his voice that made his innocence of a moment ago seem less credible and throwing an arch look into the garden where the napkin was all that remained on the lawn: "What a most enjoyable party."

Marxist Garden Gnomes

Her mother gave her a pram as a wedding present. The tall English kind. It had spent years in their attic, covered up. She had bought it for herself before the show closed down for good when she fancied that, just in the nick of time, she was pregnant. Whether it was a false alarm or whether she gave birth to a dead rabbit—she was under the spell of a white-haired travelling magician at the time—I now forget. In any case it had never been used. It came by messenger although her mother hadn't asked if she wanted it, and Olga put it straight into our junk room. In time more junk collected in and around and over it so that it was eventually hidden from sight. As she put it in there she said with irritation that her mother wanted to make sure that she too would soon be without breasts and have one of those floppy puckered bellies. At such times I could argue until I was blue in the face that she was afraid to have a baby because of that stupid, dried-up, mischief-making mother of hers saying that Olga had eaten away that breast as a baby. Or because that bitch had been continually unfaithful and left her and her father to their own fate. It didn't help. She wouldn't be talked out of her fear. She'd come back at me with stories of girl-friends who had been beauties but who turned into slack old sacks after the first child trundled behind the pram. Or that breastfeeding had given them sores and they had to pay the toll of motherhood with slashed and scarred breasts. She lost no time in dragging me off to the family planning clinic for condoms and a cap. And she used such an exaggerated quantity of spermicidal cream with the thing that it was like sticking your prick in glue. She would allow it the ordinary way only a few days per cycle. Free-lancing as it were. (Allow wasn't really the word for it. She cringed with fear when she thought there was even the remotest danger. It simply wouldn't work then. She couldn't get her legs apart.) Three days before her period and a few days after. During she didn't care for much. She called it the blood wedding and was always most concerned when I had difficulty washing the blood clots out of my pubic hair and my scrotum. The rest of the time the artificial rubber hymen was inserted to prevent the tadpoles from begetting the next generation. And when she was fertile, which she could gauge almost down to the hour with her thermometer, it wasn't allowed at all. Not even if I had lumped ten condoms one on top of the other and all the plastic bags and gum boots in the house over my cock. But I must admit that on those occasions she offered me an understudy for her cunt that could pass muster. Her beautiful round arse (she had briefly had an Italian boyfriend).

63

She would lie on her stomach after the playing and teasing and say sweetly while parting her cheeks and showing me that heavenly rose-brown pooper of hers: "Put it in here, my love." Then I'd quickly go to the kitchen to hang my cock in salad oil for easier sliding. Moments later I'd be on her and looking down along her speckled back and the magnificent rounding of her hips I watched how that rod of mine kept disappearing between those two spherical, fair hills (her tail had only a few freckles). And she came like any other time. Music and all. She always said: "I can feel it through the inside. It's about the same." I had to waste no time washing the shit from between my foreskin or I'd have a swollen top the next morning like the backlight on a bicycle. When we were thus engaged we always played that I was an Inca priest offering up a maiden. I let her throw her head back so her neck was taut and we pretended that at the moment I filled her a priestess cut her stretched throat with one stroke of a razor-sharp knife. When these games excited her more than usual she turned her head, opened her mouth and said that I must spit in her. When I came. Because my spit was deadly as prussic acid and would kill her on the spot. When she received both deposits at the same time she almost erupted with excitement. And so we lived, despite her panic about pregnancy, a very happy and exciting life. I didn't want one of those screaming tit-suckers in the house yet. My work kept my hands full for the time being, because it wasn't easy to start off as a sculptor in a city that had been planted deep with the Marxist garden gnomes of a previous generation. They were everywhere. On the bridges. Stuck to houses. By urinals. In sandstone, in limestone and in granite. Wee mannikins. Bald-pated dwarfs, usually with bared chests.

64

Workers, they were supposed to be, portraying the nobility of work. But one of my colleagues once said, whispering: "That's not human socialism. That's socialism for apes." No matter, these proletarian Neanderthalers were none of my business for a while. My job was to render Happy Motherhood in bronze for a city park. It would have to be a mother with a child of course if the broad hints of the Commission for the Beautification of the City were anything to go by: "These days they tend to make what they call abstracts, women looking like a big balloon, which is then called Primordial Mother or something of the sort. A trend we are averse to," one of the commission members had said casually. I had tried to win them over to the idea of a pregnant woman but they thought that a rather premature happy Motherhood. Anyway, I couldn't very well have tied a cushion to Olga's stomach under her clothes when she posed. She would have died of misery, as she said herself. To hold the big doll I had bought at the toyshop nearby (a bargain because it was Damaged Stock), was hard enough for her. She stood with it for months, sometimes six hours a day. But if it was at all possible, as when I was working on the back of the statue, she'd quickly put it by her feet. On its dented face. When the figure was finished and the Commission came to look at it, they were all very enthusiastic with the exception of one grey-headed functionary who spoke the prophetic words: "It looks as if that mother is afraid of her child." It was true. She was glad when it left the house to be cast in bronze at the foundry and she never came with me to see the place where it was put, to the park by the canal among all the mothers with prams and toddlers. Among the genuine motherhood. She wanted the cracked and unfinished studies in clay and plaster out of the house too. I didn't want to put them out for the dustman because I knew I would only wind up looking through the windows to see them back on the mantlepieces of my neighbours. That's when the pram came into its own. We pulled all the mess off it and out of it and loaded it high with miniature mothers and children till it almost went through the springs. One evening we wheeled it up the bridge over the Amstel. Perhaps we even sang some appropriate nursery rhymes. When we reached the middle of the bridge I wanted to wait until there were no cars coming by in case they thought we were drowning a child. But she started plopping them in the water straight away. One after the other and as far out as possible. I was left out of it altogether. And then I saw the doll bobbing up and down below. She had saved it for last. When it was done she lightheartedly pushed the pram home, letting it roll down the bridge and running after it. It was a very happy sight. A young mother acting like a spring lamb. But once at home she rode it straight into the junk room and hid it under the paraphernalia again. Now that we had a clean ship I could begin on her by herself. With the money that was left over from the commission I could, if we were careful, work for myself for a year. She spent almost that entire year walking about the studio naked. I did her sitting, standing, lying and in a dance pose with her arms horizontal and one leg in the air. They call it a pretty name in ballet, arabesque, she told me. But you could look straight into her cunt. I made her as Pomona with apples that she kept finishing off while posing. *Scrapple from the Apple*. As Persephone with wild flowers from the field that she picked herself. Whence the small green caterpillars and the froghoppers crawled out over her heavenly body. I hewed a torso of her in granite that disappeared

66

into the garden of a rich old bugger, because if you can't get the woman you have to make do with stone. And I made hundreds of drawings of her. I knew every inch of her body in the end. I had traced every curve, every dimple, every crease with my eyes. My hands had followed in clay. I was like the insects from the bouquet from the field that crept over her, for whom her breasts were mountains to cross and who could find shade in the valley between her shoulder-blades. And in the intervals when she was on the toilet I made sketches of ourselves making love in a variety of ways. I wrote on them "DON'T BE LONG! I'M GOING TO DO THIS WITH YOU." Or: "I'M GOING TO OFFER YOU UP." When she was unbearably irresistible, especially so if she was fertile (you could tell simply by looking at her she was so like a flower in full bloom). I wrote: "I LOVE YOU SO MUCH, DON'T WIPE YOUR ARSE, I'LL LICK YOU CLEAN." She never took me up on it. She always imagined it was a figure of speech. Poetic exaggeration. Meanwhile she managed to look after the house in a fantastic way. We didn't have much money to spend on food but she could fillet and do a steamed mackerel with sauce over it and all sorts of things around it so well that it made you look around for the waiter to ask which wine should best be drunk with this. And she filled the studio with bowls of fruit. Mixed with the fusty smell of the clay it was just like we lived in an orchard. When she bought leeks she rinsed them and laid them side by side on the blocks of stone for a day before we ate them. The same with all the vegetables. Because she thought it was such a pity to take one of those beautiful white cauliflowers, cut it up and devour it straight away. Or she brought in a big bag of pickling onions and would sit on the balcony all day, peeling them in the wind, her eyes red from weeping. Then the street was blown full of silver skins and the heady wine aroma of dried bay leaf hung inside. In a few days the cupboard in the studio would be filled with jars of onions in vinegar, with bay leaves, red peppers and cloves. In among her portraits and figures. With her forehead still sweating from the effort she looked it over and said with deep satisfaction: "The winter store." A warm mood of wood-gathering then settled over the studio. As though we lived in a hut *(Full many a glorious morning have I seen)* at the edge of the dunes under trees grown crooked against the wind from the sea, with fly-banes and earths stars all about. As though if we weren't careful we could fall vicitim to the elements. And the neighbours and everyone could see her constant sweet way in making everything cosy and warm because at a party I overheard a neighbour say behind my back: "Such a beautiful girl, always out to please and coddle him. I don't know what he does with her, but the chap must have a golden prick." When I had been working like this for a year, obsessed by her and her body, I received another commission. For a building of the Red Cross. It seemed as if the devil had a hand in it as they wanted another mother and child. She said straightaway that she wasn't having anything to do with it. She didn't want to pose for it. She might get sick, die, or leave me. But I would never get her to stand with one of those gruesome dolls in her arms again. I had better do without a model. Which I did. Thus one may see that domestic circumstances can play an important role in the development of art. (Lard pour l'art). I made a larger-than-life bent figure, open, picking a rudimentary child, though it was really more of a creature really, off the ground. The statue expressed a motherly gesture rather than the relationship between a woman and child. No breasts, its body a hole through which you'd be able to see the grass in which it was to stand and a face without human expression. Her clenched fist was on the ground. Olga loved it. She was enthusiastic. Too enthusiastic. Because it had nothing to do with her. Perhaps because she felt it had nothing to do with any mother and child. That's why she worked like a horse when the plaster-cast was made. She walked around in jeans and a work shirt with a scarf tied around her head and her face and arms covered with white spatters, so that she looked like a combination of a bricklayer, a plasterer and a female construction worker from Russia. She helped me take the clay from the forms, make buckets of plaster. The sweetheart! All the seams and crinkles of her body were white. And her red hair was grey with dust. When the figure was cast in bronze and placed, I received an invitation to attend the official opening of the building—by the Queen. Saying it was intended that "the artist be introduced to Her Majesty on the site of his accomplishment." Olga and I went into fits of laughter because in the studio we had done a lot of screwing in the shadow of the statue and thus had achieved one accomplishment after the other. She went off at once to make a new dress. She cut it so low that she kept coming up to me, bending forward a little, to ask if I could see anything: "Just the nipples," I'd say. Which was the truth. So on the day of the opening we stood in the warm autumn sunshine at our post by my statue. She looked so beautiful that I didn't care a bugger for my statue. Behind the windows we could see the Queen waft through the various departments of the building, dribbled on by a retinue of morning-coated marabous who kept taking a few steps back to let her go

69

in front. As if she had to try out the strength of the floor. A little later we saw her walk over the grounds, tarry by the ornamental lake and apparently waving at the pelicans on the little island. And I believe they actually nodded back with their vacuum cleaner sacks. Possibly because Her Majesty was wearing something outlandish with feathers on her head again. They thought she was one of theirs. Then they came in our direction. Olga cutting the air beside me like a figure-head with three-quarters of her breasts on the serving platter of her corselet. But when the procession of black ants and their queen drew near, they curved away and passed us. Later, on the terrace, when the royal guest had long been carried away in a shiny black ceremonial car and everyone could hoist sherry to his greedy heart's content and Olga had just gone to the ladies leaving me standing in a corner alone, a bustling little inquisitorial master of ceremonies came up to me. He regarded me with disapproval and said: "You understand that under these circumstances we couldn't present you to Her Majesty." When I raised my eyebrows in surprise he added, whispering: "The way the lady in your company is dressed is beyond the pale." A few years after she left me I happened to pass by that statue and I stopped and sat down opposite it by the side of the ditch, as the gateway to the building was closed. I saw that whole September day again. How she stood there in the tight dress with those tits of hers rising over it like dahlias floating in a bowl. How she put my statue in the shade. A lifeless piece of abstraction that had nothing of her. And it hit me all of a sudden that I, with this figure, had given shape to her fear. Her fear of motherhood. That it wasn't a woman lifting a child but pushing it away from her to the earth. That the dimensions of the child exactly fitted the hole that was the woman's body. And that it had to do with her after all, the way I had seen her recently. After what had become of her. Damaged, after two abortions by a grubby needlewoman, minus one ovary and weary from running away from herself. And I was frightened by the figure I had made, which she, carefree and happy, had helped me with. Because I must have looked into the future with a terrible clarity. But what my hands had already known, I myself understood too late. Too late to be able to help her any more.

Peel Me a Grape

Of course she was vain. What do you expect when men almost walk into trams to follow you with their eyes, when a concert of car horns accompanies you doing the shopping and the women in the neighbourhood would love to burn you at the stake because their men stay by the window with a hand in their trouser pocket until you return from the butcher's. When she went to Bata's in the Kalverstraat for shoes she often bought them too small. She would tell me that her feet were swollen from shopping too long. But it was easy to see by the meat cushions of her instep (the nether tits) what was going on. Later, when it hurt her to walk, she would admit I was right. That she was just like one of Cinderella's stepsisters. Then I turned the bench vice open and said I could

71

easily take off a bit of heel or toe with the hacksaw. Or I went after her with a pair of sharp wire cutters. And once, walking home on a Sunday morning at four o'clock from a midnight concert—Jay Jay Johnson and Lee Konitz—the blood stood in her shoes. The pigeons cooed like crazy in the trees of the Van Baerlestraat but didn't let on whether she was the bride the prince was seeking. At first she walked a little way on her bare feet, hunched with pain, but she couldn't keep it up for long. Anyway, she was afraid she might put her broken blisters into some old man's green-yellow gob. I said I'd carry her home. First she tried to hang her plump softness in my arms but that proved to be impossible. I was no Johnny Weissmuller and she was no Jane. Then she pulled up her tight skirt and jumped on my back. And every time some drunken tomcat overtook us he'd stop and let us pass again. Because the wee little silk thing she wore had quite disappeared up her grand canyon so she would appear to be riding in her bare bum and that, even for someone stupid with booze and dying to hit the sack, was a sight for sore eyes in the first rosy light of the new Sunday. To wonder at. In that period we went to all the jazz concerts, even if we had to do without meat for a week. Art Blakey and the Jazz Messengers with Lee Morgan on trumpet. The Miles Davis Quintet. Jazz from Carnegie Hall: Dizzy Gillespie, Roy Eldridge, Stan Getz. The Sonny Rollins Trio. Max Roach and his All-Stars. Tens of meals of just potatoes and vegetables. If it finished at an hour when the only people abroad were men going fishing and her shoes were large enough to enable her to stand on her own legs, we played The Car I'll Buy When I'm Rich down the long Churchill-Laan, just so we wouldn't notice how slowly the miserable flagstones moved under our feet. If we passed, say, a humble Volkswagen, she would say: "You'll give me the tenth car after this one when you're rich and famous." She imagined that it would be only a matter of a few years. If it turned out to be a Citroen DS or a Jaguar she was elated as a child. She'd kiss me on both cheeks as if I'd just put it there for her. And if it was somebody's rusty darling ready for the pile, or a crumpled old pet, she said that we must have made a mistake in counting. That we had to start all over again. Because she couldn't be expected to take her French handmade, Charles Jourdan shoes that cost one hundred and twenty-five guilders into a vehicle worth no more than fifty in scrap iron. We played that game in many different parts of Amsterdam since we often went to parties as well as to all the midnight performances of the film society at the Kriterion. In Alkmaar's provincial cinema she hadn't seen much besides Romy Schneider in *Sissy the Young Empress* and *High Society* with Louis Armstrong. She still sang the tunes from it, when she was washing spinach or peeling the potatoes: "Who wants to be a millionnaire? I don't. Have flashy flunkeys everywhere? I don't." She was utterly amazed at the whole world of film. She didn't understand how it was done. To her I was the magician who pulled it all out of the hat. The immense decors in Griffith's *Intolerance*. The heads of the Assyrians that had rolled so realistically into the auditorium that you felt like looking for them between the seats at the end of the film. She worked herself against me as we shuddered at Conrad Veidt or Boris Karloff. Or when the razor almost touched the bulging eye in *Un Chien Andalou* and the camera turned to the moon with a wisp of cloud drifting across it. The sort of thing that draws an icy shriek from one. The

73

bald Mongolian blowing into that beautiful fur in
Storm over Asia made her think of the coat I'd given
her. When I was hitchhiking and she picked me up.
She recalled that I looked just as greedy then. Not
for the fur but her. For months we called for a spoonful of soup in certain situations after seeing *Potemkin*.
But the one she loved best was *Citizen Kane* with
Orson Welles. Especially when the old man lies on
his deathbed and the glass ball with the snow storm
whirling in it falls from his dying hands and he
murmurs "ROSEBUD." Each time I stretched out
on the divan at home with a ping-pong ball and let
it fall from my hand in a faithful imitation of that
scene she was almost in tears. Probably because it
reminded her of her father's deathbed. I never told
her that the last thing he said was about those boys
who came for supper. Maybe if it had been something
attractive like "rosebud," or even "buttercup" say,
I would have told her. But life is no film, by God.
Those boys didn't go. The one that made her
laugh the most was a Mae West movie, where Mae is
at the front door of her house being treated with
disdain by a rich lady who's telling her to leave her
husband alone and Mae turns back into the house
and lets off steam by imperiously telling the maid:
"Peel me a grape." When a credit squeeze was
introduced (that feeble bunch of bunglers in The
Hague trying to stop up the leak that armament
hysteria had created in the budget) I found myself
involved in the Aid for Arts scheme. Instead of rich
and famous I became poverty-stricken and ignomi-
nious. When I tucked the few miserable notes the Aid
scheme gave us in her hand for the housekeeping
she'd make an elegant gesture and say: "Peel me a
grape." And she cheerfully went out to earn some
extra money. Welding plastic baby pants in a small

74

factory near us for a guilder an hour. If she worked from eight to twelve and came home with plastic-dust in her hair and cramp in her fingers from the piecework, but with the four guilders, she was very proud that she had earned enough money for our food for that day all by herself. When she let her money add up for a few days and worked a Saturday morning as well she often came home with a quart bottle of gin, a large bottle of cola and half a pound of salted peanuts. Then in the afternoon we'd settle down together by the open doors of the studio to drink and nibble, listening to the Charlie Parker, Miles Davis and Sonny Rollins records that I had bought from the money for supplies I received once every three months. "Slow boat to China," "How are things in Glocca Morra?" "Sipping at Bells," "Chasing the Bird." When she got a job with the Social Insurance Bank and earned much more she always brought a couple of potted plants home at the end of the week. Cacti usually. She fixed places for them in the window sill. A kind of gallery. As if those fat watery things had to have a good view of what was going on outside. Upright prickly cucumbers, reclining juicy gherkins covered with silver-grey hair. And living stones. Lumps of something (something filthy) with roots. She loved them and could spend hours looking at them, as if they were performing a ballet just for her. But to me they were just like rotten nipples or the cunt of an old ewe. When she left me and I got around to watering that army of cacti after weeks of neglect it was too late. They had dried up and shrunk and looked like croquettes after a month in the Sahara. At first they were very enthusiastic about her in the office but in the long run they couldn't afford to keep her there; her industry could not make up for the loss of man hours her appearance caused.

The head of her department kept sending her from one end of the building to the other with fake files for other heads of departments. Once, when she opened a file in the corridor, it held just a piece of paper with the message: *"Dear Adrian, Here are the goods. Look closely. Pretty, don't you think? Watch how she walks. Hup, hup, hup. You know what I mean. William."* After one of these messages they generally went off and spent some fifteen minutes in the lavatory. So she pretty well had to leave or else she would have disrupted the entire benefit machinery for the mentally disturbed and other invalids "within the meaning of the Act" as it is called. For a while that was the end of the gin and jazz. But I liked having her around me again and she stood up very well to poverty. She once told me it was cosy and snug because it gave her an opportunity to show what she could do with a smoked herring and a few tomatoes, parsley and a hard-boiled egg. But sometimes when she couldn't bear it and she longed for something sweet, she asked like a little girl: "Can I make cakes?" Then she bought fresh bread and a small package of butter. She'd sit down at the table with an eager face, greedily spread a thick layer of butter on a piece of bread and sprinkle a centimeter of grated chocolate on it and aniseed powder over that. Winter in Sweetland she called it. Or she might pour half a pot of strawberry jam on two pieces of bread, put chocolate flakes on top with a slice of pink coconut bread to cap it. Her eyes twinkling with mischief, her large mouth full of jam and chocolate bits she'd dispose of her handiwork. Her father used to let her make cakes for lunch when she came home and her mother was out with the girls. He would start on his own ration of two thin slices of bread and two slivers of cheese that she'd left on the sink for him. But watching

Olga as she tucked in he would weaken quickly and whisper, as if an evil genii lurked behind the door: "Make me a cake too?" And when he'd greedily disposed of three or four he'd wipe the crumbs from his plate onto Olga's saying: "Don't tell mama, will you?" So she could have as many cakes as she wanted as far as I was concerned. Instead of going to jazz concerts and films we sometimes visited Mother Nature, who doesn't charge admission. Places that nearly all disappeared about the same time she did. Pumped full of sand and filled with flats. The Zuidelijke Wandelweg with the orange tennis courts behind tall elders and tottering shacks and vague sheds. The school gardens, where children grubbed in the black boggy earth of small vegetable beds. The greenhouse roofs splashed with slops of whitewash made it seem as if there was a colony of herons in the trees overhead. The flowers you could pick yourself for fifty cents. As many as you could carry. This gave me the idea to make that large Persephone of her. The fen where golden-rod grew in the autumn between the rushes which little boys picked in big sheaves for their mothers if they were going to come home with wet and muddy feet. There was usually a couple of boys calling out from a hut they had made as we came by arm in arm: "Come on, give her a kiss!" And once, they were so giggly we thought it was a joke: "Mister! Lady! There's a man here who wants to feel our wiener! How dirty can you get?" But then we noticed a little pip-squeak of a fellow pushing off through the rushes towards his bike and riding off as fast as he could go. The Buitenveldertse Wandelweg went through the lower marshland and by the clearwater ditches where even in the heart of summer the imagination saw dark, bent figures leaving the city on skates and swarming out

77

over the polders. The twists in the path which was grown over with willow shoots where benches stood and where she had so often kicked off her shoes and stretched out in the sun with her head on my lap, listening to the murmurs of sound from the summer cottages coming through the bushes. That's if there wasn't a little man sitting there, waiting to show his cock to any solitary nurse who might cycle by. And then the dike, where there were nearly always more peeping toms than necking couples so that the area had the appearance of a camera crew recording a love scene. The bend in the river seen from above, looking down on the cargo-boats sideslipping by, their decks full of red crates or orange oil barrels. The herons, the same colour as the water below, sailing over the ripples and the rowers' voices that travelled up as if they were very close. The trees of Amstelhaven in the distance with colonies of crows rising into the air as if the treetops had suddenly expanded. There, by the elbow of the river she once ate all seven ice lollies I had bought for her from the icecream man by the rusty bicycle shed next to the Miranda Pool. It gave her cramps of course and she went home doubled up with her hands pressed to her stomach. Years later when everything between her and me was long gone and hopelessly lost she still remembered all these everyday things when she suddenly dropped in to say hello. I made her come with me for a walk to the dike that night. I hadn't been there myself for years either. The earthworks all around were now almost at a level with the dike. The high privets had gone and deep bulldozer tracks ran through the ground. There was a fire of old suitcases and torn chesterfields and all the other things that eventually end up on waste land. She stood so close that her skin tightened with the heat and said: "Fire is the most beautiful of all." And then we looked up at the tall fences of lighted windows and I tried to show her where everything used to be, but I didn't know myself. On the way back she said that on the first of January, six years before, we had eaten lamb with butterbeans. And apricots afterwards. And it reminded me of what a friend had said in a letter shortly after she went: "You two were so bloody happy and it just came to an end."

A Mouse with a Trauma

She wasn't afraid of spiders or mice. One summer's evening when the cat came in with a mouse between her teeth—the tail was hanging out in an elegant coil so that she looked like Salvador Dali—Olga took it from her straight away. The cat probably just wanted to play with it because there was nothing wrong with the little thing. It was merely soaked with cat slobber and one ear had crumpled against its head. We put him in a bucket on some scraps of newspaper and left him there to get his breath back. When we looked in on him after a few hours he was sitting in his beautiful downy fur pelt—you felt like blowing on it like the Mongolian in *Storm over Asia,* that's how beautiful it was—on his haunches, washing his face. His ear had uncrumpled and he immediately ate pieces of bread from my hand. We wanted to let him recover from his fright for a day or so before letting him go. The next morning, before setting him free, we were taking a last look at Jonathan (as Olga had christened him) when the cat suddenly appeared between us, curious, put her paws on the sides of the bucket and peered down. And instantly, like pulling the tendon of a chicken claw, the ear crumpled back against the mouse's head. When we pushed the cat away, the ear re-formed as if someone had waved a wand. Now Olga wanted to keep him. She thought it was fascinating to have a mouse with a trauma for a pet. But after a few days I was able to persuade her to push the animal through a mousehole underneath the sink, as he kept jumping up the sides of the bucket and falling back with a little plop. Later I heard that he probably died a terrible death. That mice do away with strangers of their own kind who enter their territory. And that they don't just go for the throat and kill, but eat the intruder as well, beginning simply anywhere in their haste to dispose of it. (Ye shall eat the fat of the friend). It is said that people who can't have children or don't want them for one reason or another fill the void with animals. Olga had not been with me a month before she wanted a cat. I was buying vegetables one day in the Albert Cuyp market when I saw a kitten standing up against the window of the pet shop. I parked my bicycle and inspected the fluffy creature carefully. Its markings were black and red, the red of Olga's hair. It had a light tip at its tail and a light stripe ran from its forehead to its nose, giving it the look of a little hussy. But in profile the tiny head was noble as a tiger's. As I have already raised the subject of mice with psychosomatic symptoms, I can now admit that the split character manifested in the cat's appearance made me decide to buy it for her. Because it was like her. Also because it meowed so pitifully when I tapped on the window, and because all that separated it from the three meatball pups who were romping wildly and scaring it was a piece of chicken wire. She was mine for a couple of guilders. It was raining so I tucked her under my jacket against my chest. On the way she crept across my shoulder and down my arm. When I got her home and told Olga to sit down because I had a surprise for her I was able to shake the kitten out of my sleeve onto her lap. She hugged me with the kitten between us and was off to buy a brush for shiny coats and separate dishes for meat and fish and catfood. After a while the cat became so attached to her that she heard the click clack of high heels and rapid step that said she was coming even before I did. And if she left the door open when she went shopping the cat followed her and sat waiting at the street corner until she returned. Even when Olga had been gone a year she still walked to the door when she heard a quick rhythm of high heels approach. This often threw me into confusion at first and I would tremble with tension imagining it was her. But they always passed, those footsteps. Then the cat stopped listening, she had given up. I believe she suffered more from the abruptness of Olga's disappearance than I did. Auburn Olga. Olga of the animals. *Potnia theiroon*, ruler of animals— our art history professor would say while he was expounding on a picture of Artemis lifting a catlike being by the scruff of the neck with each hand. If one could indeed stride through her life in seven league boots one would stride from one animal event to another. Beginning with cats. Because "cat" soon became "cats". Once the puss became an adult she was pregnant twice a year. Basketsful of young. Small red toms, black females and all shades in between with cat lounging on her side presenting those red nipples, and troupes of young drinking themselves blotto. One time—it was the kind of sultry August day when the heat seems to stand on top of you—the cat was giving birth and the last one got stuck so Olga had to pull it out herself. But the cat kept panting faster and faster and had no interest at all in her litter. In the middle of the night we had to take her in a taxi to the vet. It turned out that there was another of her young inside, dead, and already decomposing because of the heat. She had to be operated on straight away. I sat in the sweltering waiting room with my arm around Olga's damp body, when the smell of ether came in through the hall. She winced at the smell as it told us the operation had started. Suddenly there was a loud thunderclap and the poplars in the dark at the back of the garden began to sway even though there seemed to be no wind. Then the rain pelted down. She was sure that it was too late to save her cat, that something had gone wrong, a feeling which was intensified by the glare of white lightning on the gardens, so that for the fraction of a second you saw trees as you'd never seen them before. Like the dirty-work-at-the-cross-roads effects in an old B movie. But then the vet appeared in the doorway laughing, wearing a bloodied apron over his striped pyjamas. We could come and have a look at the cat. She was lying in a cage set over her on the operation table. Wet and dishevelled, and still unconscious. She had a bald, pale pink patch on her stomach and the flesh had been drawn together so it looked like a stuffed roast. The vet said we could collect her in a week's time and before we left Olga embraced him and placed a resounding kiss on each of his cheeks for sacrificing so much of his night's rest. I imagine that he lost the rest of it too. That was the cat. Now for the pigeons. She came home one day from the Amstelveld poultry market with them: two sand-coloured turtle doves with a black band around the neck. I immediately set to and made a house for them with blue perches and shell-sand on the floor. At first I quite liked all that cooing and they were a sexy pair: they often screwed more than we did. And afterwards they'd laugh and giggle so gleefully that they made you feel like some more yourself. There was something poetic about it too. The young married couple much in love on the bed, their nakedness partly covered by the sheets and the sound of cooing doves. But the loveplay of this wanton pair had its usual consequence as inside of a few months the female was sitting on two white eggs. Olga couldn't leave the eggs alone. She would keep listening to them and one day she said she heard a soft tapping. She thought they would hatch tiny and beautifully feathered birds. Something like plump wrens or little chicks. But one morning there were two of these disgusting bald bags of guts with prehistoric heads in the nest. She was terribly disappointed. It nauseated her when the parents retched the half-digested food into them with heaving noises. They looked more gruesome as they got bigger. They became bluer and more wizened-looking day by day and a mess of intestines and veins rampaged through them like a disease. She told me they had to go. I know why. I never asked her, but it was undoubtedly because of that cancerous tit of her mother's. That's certainly what I thought of every time I looked at those knotted balls of innards held together by a wrinkled membrane. When a friend came to see us and just loved it all, Olga was glad to sell them to her at a loss. She never mentioned those lustful gigglers again. After the pigeons came the tree

83

frogs. Green as moss, and they did at least keep their mouths shut. Sometimes one of them might blow up the dirty-white bladder under his throat but I never heard it come to a croak. She kept them in a glass tank and a few times a week she put in branches of fresh leaves and fed them mealworms which she tried to keep as fresh as possible by standing the jar under running water. She often sat and watched the animated pink clump in the jar with all its vibrating ends and once she said that if there was a soul that's what it would probably look like. One time when the tinkling of water which was like rain constantly gurgling through the gutters annoyed me and I turned the tap off, the sea anemone-like clump changed to meat coloured mud overnight. A more likely picture of the soul. Sometimes she'd put a treefrog in her hand to let it jump for a plant. Or we ran broadjumping competitions with them as if they were toys. But they mostly lived a forgotten existence by the window of the junk room because it was a struggle to get past the pram to reach them. When she left me and I was in bed for weeks numb with misery, the cat managed to push the wire top off the glass tank. They escaped and later on I found them here and there between the junk, dried up. They were still quite recognizably frogs, but hard as celluloid. Then there was the weasel. I saw it walk by when I put my head around the corner of my studio door. I was after it at once. After the flashing brown stripe that disappeared through a door that was standing ajar. When I carefully opened the door a little wider and looked inside, a little face with two dark eyes peeped at me from behind a dustpan and brush. I called Olga, grabbed an empty dustbin from the side of the road and told her to hold it in front of the open door after I went in. When I shouted she was to set it upright quickly and slam the lid on. Then I went inside. The smart little eyes again looked at me for a moment but then disappeared. I stole into the corner and tapped on the dustpan. A brown arrow darted for the open door. I shouted to Olga and heard the clang of the dustbin lid at the same time. It all happened so quickly that she hadn't seen anything. We didn't know if the weasel was inside. We took the dustbin to the studio and when I opened it he jumped up, clearing the rim by at least a foot. But straight up, fortunately, so he plopped back into the bin. Lid back on like lightning, a plug of cotton wool with ether, and then I had the little creature by the skin of the neck, the white of his stomach hanging down like a greasy cravat. We laid him in the old pigeon house and he soon recovered his wits and began to eat the minced steak I pressed on the end of a paint brush and stuck through the bars. He must have been starved because he ate a hamburger's worth in one sitting. Olga wanted to keep him and would have opened the cage to stroke him for a minute. But I told her not to, that she needed all ten fingers to weld plastic baby pants. That you shouldn't keep such a creature in a cage, that it was torture for him. I went off to the neighbours for a glass tank to transport him on my bicycle and set him free somewhere in the countryside. Olga was to keep an eye on him in the meantime. When I returned she was desperate. She had left to get the mail from the letterbox and when she came back to the studio he had escaped. I couldn't believe it. There was a bare half inch of space between the bars and nowhere were they bent nor could I see pieces of fur. We turned the studio upside down, but not a trace of him anywhere. I thought that he might possibly have escaped through a small hole in the

85

floor or even a mouse hole. Later, when I was shifting blocks of stone in the studio, I half-expected him to be between them, all dried out and flattened and that he would fall over like a piece of cardboard. When the big radiator that provided us with central heating had to be moved for painting two years later and Olga could at last clean up all the junk that had fallen behind it in the course of years—pieces of plaster from before the war, rusty wire, a small piece of canvas with a clumsy oil painting of a couple of birds—she came up to me solemnly and dramatically with a redbrown something cupped in her hands. I almost had a fit because I thought her hair had fallen out. But it was the remains of the little weasel. Some parchment-like skin that shed fur when you touched it. Not even worth a funeral. It went into the dustbin with the rusty wire in which it had become entangled and the other mess, without so much as a goodbye. Then came a sweet little companion who when he was killed in a horrible accident was given a real funeral. With flowers and tears and all. He was borne solemnly in a cigar box on the back of the bicycle. I dug a hole with my hands under a large, airy ash tree in the Amsterdam Wood and put the little box in it and Olga, sobbing, laid the orchid on it she had bought with her own money (it cost five guilders, five hours welding baby pants). It hurt me to sprinkle the sand over it, not because that dear black and white duck was lying, crushed, in the cigar box but because the orchid was being buried alive. I had to hold her up or she would have fallen in the stinging nettles on the forest floor. We always went to the isle of Ameland for our holidays and we used to tuck into the little bottles of sherry in the Restaurant Car of the train to Leeuwarden and so were quite sozzled on the boat from Holwerd. On a camping ground right behind the dunes we'd hire a tent-house made of whitewashed wood to shoulder level with the rest canvas so that a wondrous light entered. Tea-coloured and warm when the sun shone and a clear peppermint if the sky was cloudy. There were miles of beach where no one came but the two of us, where we walked naked all day and where she could sit her beautiful bum down on me and ride me in a shallow pool. Or could let me fuck her on a sand bank in the sun between bubble weed and blue jelly fish with purple frilled petticoats. That's where I took that picture of her lying on her back in the loose sand with the wild roses I had put in her hair. Her breasts were pointing straight up, which once made someone ask: "Is that for real?" I didn't reply, because she had long gone from me and those breasts of hers, those lovely, hard and yet soft things had grown flaccid through her stupid, messy way of life, her boozing and her night-owling. And there, in the dunes, she found the little shel-duck. He followed her as I have read they do when they have lost their mother. The first living being they meet becomes their mother, whether it is a beautiful woman like Olga or a fisherman with bent, hairy legs and nails filthy from scratching around in seaweed. That sweet fuzzy creature with the black and white markings had been in luck. From the post office in Nes I telephoned a biologist who said it was possible to keep them alive with bits of fresh fish and shrimps. But that they needed mother warmth at night. That was a problem as you could let them sleep on your chest, but that meant being shitted upon. When they're with the mother the whole kit and caboodle sleeps underneath her with their works pointing outwards. When one of them has to take a shit he squeaks and before the muck squirts out the mother has raised herself so her feathers aren't used for toilet paper. I related all this to Olga, who was sitting at the table with her arms spread wide while the duck went back and forth in between them. She said that it was worth it. And so she went to sleep each evening on her back with that little thing between her breasts. Sometimes, I woke up early and looked at her lying there as if she had three breasts. Two ordinary ones of nice, pink human flesh and another in between dressed in downy fur for winter. Before going to sleep she wound a cloth around his tailpiece and that usually worked, but he sometimes managed to twist himself out and when he did she awoke with a pair of breasts that looked like the udder of a goat who's been lying in mud. With those soiled tits bare she then ran right across the slumbering, early morning tent camp to the sea and rinsed them clean in the salt sea, where I had been earlier with a shrimp net to catch small sole, plaice and shrimp for the duckling. When a couple of shel-ducks passed overhead in powerful, majestic flight I told her he would be like that one day. It made her sad because she realized that she would have to let him go when the time came. And he worked hard at it himself because he grew so fast that we needed a box to take him back to Amsterdam at the end of the holiday. He now had little wings which he flapped dapperly, stretching himself as if already trying out the sails of freedom. He followed Olga everywhere. He caused traffic jams following her to the baker's down the street. And in the studio, where I was working at a statue of Olga with a cat in her arms, he trampled around in the pools on the floor when I had hosed the clay, as though sea-worms would come up out of the concrete. And that was how the fatality occurred. While I was backing

88

away to look at the statue and Olga from a distance, I stepped on him. There was a creaking as if he had a wooden framework inside him. He lay twitching at my feet and Olga screamed and writhed. The rest of the day she sat against the wall with the dead bird between her body and her drawn-up legs and cried. Once in a while I sat down beside her and put my arm around her and blubbered too. But she was inconsolable. I think that's why the figure of the woman with the cat had such tenderness. Because she posed for it so sadly and the grief stayed with her for months. And in contrast to what the commissioner said of my woman and child figure: "It seems as if that woman is afraid of her child", someone on the City of Groningen Committee, which bought the woman and cat, remarked: "The woman holds that cat as if it is her child." After Olga left me, the plaster cast of that statue stood in open air exhibitions all over the country. When she'd call in after the second or third broken marriage, she'd say, not without pride: "I have seen myself again. With the cat. In Rotterdam on the Lijnbaan." When it was cast in bronze and I had sold it, I came home late one night and found her standing like a white shadow by my studio door. It startled me so much that it took quite a while before I understood that the foundry had returned the plaster cast and not finding anyone at home had left it by the door. I had to support myself on the figure for a while before all the emotions receded and I had the strength to lug it inside and put it in the place where it belonged. Where it has remained. To this day.

Miss Waspwaist

What happened? With her, with Olga? What
changed over the years? Or had I been blind to
something that always existed? Had I failed to see
the dear red animal trying to free herself from my
embrace—with hesitation in the beginning and hardly
noticeable, but ever more vehemently as time went
on? With all my longing and despair I kept asking
myself these questions over and over again when
she first left me. Because it wasn't true of course what
I used to say later on, that if I hadn't taken a telephone
she would never have left me. Coming home I would
find her more and more frequently on the phone to
her mother. This wasn't so strange, especially after
the death of her father, but that she always finished
talking and put the telephone down as soon as I
came in made me suspicious in the long run. I also
noticed that afterwards she seemed put out. Sort
of discontented. She'd sit with a book in her lap but
didn't read. And if I asked her what she was thinking
about she said: "Oh nothing, nothing in particular."
And then she quickly read on. But if I looked up
from my work a little later she'd be staring again.
It would often come out during dinner. One of her
girlfriends had been to see her mother in her own
little car, a birthday present from her husband. And
she'd been raving about all the trips she'd made
through Europe. And the cupboards full of clothes
she could choose from when she went into the city
in the afternoons to meet friends. I knew precisely
how her mother had talked. The calculating slut.
In that honeyed voice, so apparently without design.
She knew how to administer the poison. At first

I tried to joke her out of it. That after only a year of marriage the Nancy in question looked pale and dissatisfied and had third-rate sagging tits and varicose veins on the limp calves of her legs because her husband was impotent from manager-disease. And that such a pale frump couldn't possibly have a dress as pretty as the one Olga had made from the material I'd just bought. And that she wouldn't like me to be the assistant director of a margarine plant giving people skin rashes with an inferior product. Travelling through Europe and stuffing one's wardrobes to bursting point with jackets and stoles of dyed rabbit fur acquired at the expense of someone else's itch. That I at least had earned the material for her dress with my own two hands and not deducted it from the pay of two hundred men at the works. That was true enough, because while she was out at work a refined and fragile silver-haired art connoisseur had bought a drawing from me. Not, however, before bringing the price down by fifty guilders, as is the custom. I was on my bike and off to the Bijenkorf, where I had been watching the material in the window for a long time. It had a pink, red, brown and dark-yellow stripe. Back at my studio I made a cardboard stencil of the outline of her body and strengthened it with wood so it could stand by itself. Then I draped the material around it and glued a piece of paper on the neck on which I wrote MISS WASPWAIST, as I often had to put my knee against her stomach and pull with all my might to get her belt one hole tighter. When she came home she blushed with delight. She picked the whole thing up, walked it to the mirror and held it before her. It covered her exactly, she was sheltering behind her own image. It was as though she had the dress on already. And she said, with wonder in her voice:

91

"How well you know the way I am." When, tongue between teeth and body full of pin pricks, she had finished making the dress, she put it on for the first time and she presented herself to me, arms held away from her sides, I said: "Olga, you are the fairest in the land. You are as beautiful as a polished apple." Later, when searching for those goddamned tree frogs, I came across the cardboard silhouette of her body among the junk and I took it out with me to the mirror and stood beside it. I laid my hands on her hips and stared at our image in the mirror. I felt and saw that material again and I tried to imagine her as she was then. But I kept seeing her as she had become and if I shook off that image I was left with only the outline. A stencil, a shadow of her. A blueprint of our happiness that needed filling in. Or was it nothing but a brown piece of cardboard? But it was more than the venomous phone calls from her mother that eventually drove her away from me. The seed that grew into the jungle enveloping her whole life had been sown early. I think it had been especially disastrous for her to see her father the way she did, the way she'd been forced to see him. Because her mother had squashed him to such an extent that there was nothing left but a fat slug of a boy with a sweet tooth. When she came through the hall with the soup-tureen he would take a quick peep inside and then, clumsily but mischievously, skip along in front of her chanting: "Soup with meat balls. Meat balls. Meat balls. Soup with meat balls. Hoy, hoy, hoy." What choice was there, between infidelity and humiliation, but to play the clown. Once when he was lying despondently on the divan, Olga had heard him talk about her mother to an uncle: "I just act as if I'd never seen her before. As if she's an attractive woman visiting us that I've never met before. Then I don't have to ask where she's been. It makes it none of my business." And she still remembered hearing a so-called uncle at her tenth birthday party say to some-one about her mother, with a greasy laugh: "Yes, but has that little woman ever got soft hands. And don't we all know it." Even when she'd only been with me a short while she slept with her knees drawn up to her breasts and her thumb in her mouth. When she was asleep she'd push me with that beautiful backside of hers into the small strip of no-man's land at the edge of the bed where I could only stop myself from falling out if the blankets had been firmly tucked in under the mattress. At first I tried to change that by settling down between her legs after we'd fucked. And we would fall asleep cosily in and against one another. But in the middle of the night I would be awakened by a slow and intermittent, but very persistent elbowing. Moments later she was pushing me away with her arms and legs while making crying noises like a whiny child not getting its way. You could push, hit or scream, it didn't make any difference. She slept on like a log. Only when she had possession of three-quarters of the bed and had her backside on your stomach did she settle down and begin to snore peacefully with her thumb in her mouth. Olga, with all her quaint, crazy, trying, sweet, wild ways. I kept loving her madly. I see us again standing in the doorway, waiting for rain on a day in August, a day of such oppressive, stifling heat that the flies stuck to your skin from sheer exhaustion. And then it came. Huge drops that washed the street black in a matter of seconds, leaving grey circles round the trees as if dust had fallen from them. Threatening blue-grey clouds drove across the sky and a moment later the cloudburst poured down with a clap of thunder. She kicked off her shoes and walked into the deluge with her arms spread wide, until she was soaked and her skin showed through her dress. Then she came inside, got undressed and put on her bikini and went out again to lie in the gutter between the parked cars in the foot-deep, grey rainwater that was pelted full of bubbles when she let the lashing rain whip her. But she didn't scream "Oh it's so cold . . . cold . . . cold!" as she did when she used to turn the shower on cold to make her breasts firm. I poured two glasses of wine—I must have had a commission at the time—put them on a tray, took them outside with me and sat down on the side of the pavement in the pool with her. We drank the wine before too much water got into it and let the tray float around with the empty glasses on it until it was sunk by the rain which was still falling in bucketsful from the sky. She thought that the cars drove by slowly so as to avoid splashing her. The idiot. When the rain had stopped and I had wrenched the wet, snaring clothes off my body in the studio, she announced: "Now I want you to fuck me as hard as you can." While the torrent outside ran gurgling through the drains I stormed over that wet body of hers like a beast. And so, in the middle of that summer's day, wet from rain and sweat, we fell asleep entangled in one another's arms. She asked me that one other time. We'd been to *View from the Bridge* and she had loved the scene just before the interval when Marco takes the chair by the foot and holds it up to Eddie, triumphant and threatening. When we came home she asked if I could do that too. I tried but like Eddie got stuck halfway. For a few weeks I practised on the sly during my morning exercises. Finally I could do it. At breakfast I said: "Look Olga!" and I grabbed the foot of the chair and put it on the table over her

94

plate. She looked at me with admiration, as if I was some kind of inferior creature, some muscle-bound gorilla, and applauded. She pushed her chair back, stood up, pulled her pretty flowered nightie above her breasts and lay down on the bed. That was the other time she said, with full, hot lips: "Now I want you to fuck me as hard as you can." No sooner had she said that than it was done. One day, as we were walking in the woods we came across a dead rabbit that had been picked apart by crows or magpies. She bent over it and screamed, and stopped me from rooting around in it with a little stick. As we walked on she said it had scared her so because there was a bit of red string hanging out of its head, just like the bit she'd once had in her shit. She had been terrified that she had cancer. That the meat inside was rotting away. She had stirred her shit with a piece of rolled up toilet paper and found it to be a thread of roast beef. But the fear remained. The first time she visited me after she went away she said: "I think I have enormous complexes. I just don't know where they are. So I push them down. To be rid of them." A few days before our last Christmas together I bought a box of fireworks for New Year's Eve; catherine wheels, roman candles, rockets and fire crackers. As she was looking into the box she suddenly began to sob. Because another year had gone by, because she felt she was getting old. And she didn't want to celebrate it or have any part of all that sickening noise. So we cycled through the snow with the box on the back of my bicycle and into the woods one day between Christmas and New Year. And there, in broad daylight, I let off the whole mess. She, chilled, looked on from a distance at the fire crackers with their tails of sparks and smoke smothering in the snow. I couldn't

even persuade her to light one of the pinwheels
I had hammered on to a tree trunk. On New
Year's Eve we went to bed at eleven o'clock and
when all hell broke loose outside she was twisting
and turning restlessly beside me and talking in her
sleep. This is how our new year began. The year
I was to lose her for ever. Olga; Miss Waspwaist.

The Anatomical Posture

All I have left over from that whole mess is the
copy of a letter from my solicitor to Olga saying that
she declares that she has taken cognizance of a request
concerning the obtainment of permission to institute
a requisition for divorce on grounds of adultery
committed by her, and which shall be lodged by her
husband with the R.H. President of the District
Court at Amsterdam. That she states that she is
acquainted with the contents of above request and
has no intention of protesting the adjudication of the
petition contained therein, and moreover agrees to
forego any summons to appear before the conciliation
board. It all began with the Household Exhibition
in the R.A.I. They had actually wanted me to make
a lifesize Hermes for their stand. For free. That's
why nothing came of it. It brought her mother to
my studio with the new manager—the third since
her father's death—a bandy-legged, hairy lump
of baboon who resembled one of the Three Stooges

96

(the worst of them). He did a lot of talking, his big jaws going hell for leather, but I couldn't understand a word of it. The only sounds he seemed to emit were "Waoh... waoh... waoh...," and it wouldn't have surprised me if he had beaten his chest as well. She had to repeat what he said. That it was child's play for me to make the statue. That they were prepared to pay for the plaster and the gilt and the rest of the expenses. Then that ape started up with his "Waoh... waoh..." again. And again she repeated what he'd said with that patient, false little smile of hers. That I musn't forget the staff, and the wings on the ankles. And it was very important that it should be lifesize. Then they'd be all right. Their stand and its shining gilt figure would dominate the entire exhibition. He boomed with laughter, his lips stretched tight over the great teeth in that enormous jaw, when I said that in Greek mythology Hermes was the god of thieves as well as commerce. He danced about in his chair with mirth, his arms flopping up and down. I discovered later that he was quite a childish man, with little imagination. Not harmless though, as he'd already been involved in several bankruptcies and had contrived to turn a cow-shed in North Holland into a kind of hanging Eastern eat-garden full of shrieking parrots and exotic mocha-coloured girls—army surplus from the colonial war. It didn't go down very well because the farmers preferred beefsteak and peas. And there wasn't going to be any life-size gilt Hermes either. My refusal had more to do with this unsavoury individual with whom I suspected she was having an affair (which turned out to be true) than being asked to work for nothing. Because if it had been Olga's father I would have put a Hermes on all four corners of the stand. Fine, they went off with their tails between their legs. She and her baboon, his hands hanging almost to his knees, thumbs out, a stance we had been taught to call the Anatomical Posture at the Academy, which made him look as though he might growl and grab someone at any moment. On the opening day of the exhibition, who should purr at me over the phone but her mother. Could she please speak to her daughter? When Olga put the phone down she wore a blush of excitement. I later suspected her dirty slut of a mother of having already mentioned the meeting she had arranged with their best client. Her mother had invited her to come and have a drink at the stand with some people from the firm to celebrate the opening. She went off at once to put on her best dress with the stripes and I stayed behind with my sculpture, my hands covered with clay so that I couldn't even hug her when she left. Towards six o'clock she phoned. Her voice now held the same excitement that her face had shown after the earlier telephone call. At that time I still blamed it on drink. They were going to eat somewhere. Did I feel like coming. Who 'they' were I could see for myself. And so I landed in an Indonesian restaurant at a long table full of people I didn't know, although Olga seemed quite at home. At least that is the impression she gave as she joined in all the superficial prattle with great enthusiasm. Sometimes I had to look to make sure it was really her sitting beside me, I felt so estranged. Meanwhile friendly Indonesian attendants in batiked head-dress bent between us and silently put bowls and dishes by our plates. The baboon raised his glass and mumbled a few sentences: "Waoh.... waoh." When his speech was prematurely applauded he viciously emptied his glass in one draught and put it down. Immediately a hectic concerto of knives and forks broke loose. Not another word was said. Everyone was swilling and stuffing. If I looked across the table I looked straight into the snout of that baboon who was stuffing his big trap with *saté* in such a revolting manner, that he looked like a reptile as he paused between swallows of his prey to recover his breath. He had mixed the various rice dishes together on his plate until it looked like an indeterminate slop of monkey vomit. I looked along the table and then it hit me that the long limp gawk sitting beside her mother because he was their best client was, across all the half-devoured meals, plates, dishes and glasses, actually flirting with my Olga. And she was flirting back. God be damned! I felt it. I could tell by the look of him. I had the feeling their legs were embracing under the table. My hands began to tremble and I couldn't get another mouthful of food down my throat. I felt the urge to ravage the feast with one pull on the tablecloth. It seemed that Olga could feel what was burning inside me. Without saying a word or daring to look at me she stood up and went to the lavatory. A moment later he went after her. I knew that he would wait for her in the dark passage next to the cloak room. That he would grab her there. I saw his filthy sweaty hands clutch into the material of her dress. I didn't know what to do. I could hardly jump him for going to the lavatory. The hostile atmosphere I sensed around me turned to whispers and giggles. I felt the complicity in all those present. I wanted to sing the "Radetzky March" at the top of my voice, her father's way: "Titty bum, titty bum, titty bum bum bum." Or to pass around the photo that stinking bitch had made of him when he was dead and lying in state and say: "A lovely picture. He looks so peaceful. Pity he moved." But I stayed numb, with my fists clenched beside my plate. I saw them

99

make their way back between the tables, and when he let her go in front past a palm tree, he touched her back as if she already belonged to him, keeping that insipid smile on his face. He walked her to her chair, pulled it back, made an elegant gesture and arranged the chair under her as she sat down. I knew with what greed he must be looking at her bum as it rolled down on the seat. There were winks and knowing laughs around the table; the little bald bookkeeper, an over-dressed cockroach who had always told her mother that such a girl from business circles was out of place in the shabby world of artists, coughed emphatically over his soup to let it be known that his logical little mind had it all worked out. It was as if I had been drained of blood. My head was ice cold, my fists clenched from the cramp in my stomach. I saw what was going to happen in the eyes of the baboon across from me before I knew it myself. His bristling eyebrows shot up, startled, and pushed the loose wrinkled skin of his forehead into his greasy thatch. Then it spurted out of me. I saw the spatters on the plates and against the glasses. And on the clothes of the people across the table. The gorilla even had a couple of coinsize pieces on his snout. A few of the women squealed and everyone laid down their cutlery and stopped chewing as the food sat behind their teeth like vomit. The batiked waiters that came running up didn't quite know how to skin this cat either. Then a wave of tomato-red mush came out of my mouth and smacked on the tablecloth like a giant pancake topped with a clearly recognizable hodge podge of meat, bean sprouts and the remains of my lunchtime fried herring, half digested by the gastric juices. A loathsome sour smell began to spread around the restaurant. Eating had stopped at all the tables now and people looked horror-stricken at the slush. Tears stood in my eyes from the filthy taste high in my nose. My chair was being tugged at and the manager asked with averted face if it wasn't time I went to the lavatory. Without wiping my face on the napkin, I stood up and made my way through the tables to the can. I knew that heads were turning with me all the way. I heard them whisper. But I saw nothing. When I was out of sight in the passage to the lavatory, I started to totter. I had to cling to the wall to stop myself from buckling at the knees. In the washroom I went over to one of the basins and leaning my arms on it for support looked into the mirror. I scared myself. A chalk-white face and eye sockets like Buster Keaton's. A dirty trail ran from the corner of my mouth to my chin. I looked myself in the eye. I thought I would die I was so solemn. Then I felt another wave rising. I didn't bend my head over the basin but just ejected it into the mirror. I didn't wait for my face to reappear through the muck sliding down. I took a gulp of water and washed the sour pieces out of my mouth. Then I walked into the corner, pulled a paper towel and wiped my face and clothes. Just then the baboon came in. He didn't see me. He made straight for the basin I'd just left. And for the first time I was able to make out what he said. He said loudly: "God damn it!" and went to the next basin. Then the little bald bookkeeper tripped in, in his bespattered finery. Behind my back I heard him say to the baboon: "Here's some more. Disgusting!" I went out and in the passage almost walked into Olga leading her mother to the ladies. She kept her head down and was simply going to pass me. All at once my fist flew out. Right in her eye. She retreated against the wall and stayed with her head down as if she didn't want to conceal with rage that she'd been the cause of it all. But her mother flailed her handbag about her and wanted to hold me back. I pushed her aside with my arm and my hand sunk into the nothingness underneath the hard cloth where that breast had been removed. And then, suddenly, I went to pieces. I dashed through the restaurant towards the exit. I heard her voice screech over the others: "That bastard!" And I got a flash of my fellow-guests all standing behind their chairs while the batik-heads sedately cleared the table. I ran through the entrance hall and was outside, when I suddenly stopped, collected myself and stepped into a taxi that had just delivered an Indonesian couple to the restaurant. At home I fell on my bed stricken with misery and I hardly knew if I'd been asleep or in a coma when she phoned me in the middle of the night. She told me that it should be obvious to me she wouldn't come home again. That she looked terrible with that black eye and that it was the second inside a few months. And so it was. Once, when we were returning from a party we were walking through the red light district and she tried to rub her drunken body against a pimp, who at once recognized a chick who would lay the golden eggs. I had a hard time pulling her away. And since he was too soft to fight she was the one to get hit in the eye. But not so hard as the second time. I froze. I told her she was welcome to stay in the hotel she was phoning from and sleep with that mother-fucker. She needn't advance the black eye for safe-conduct. And I wished her much happiness with her married slob because I had seen the bite in his finger where the creep's wedding ring had been. If she searched the pockets of his suit tomorrow morning she was bound to come across it. I'd scored a bull's eye. She threw the phone down. Then my rage and anguish discharged themselves in destruction. One by one I seized the portraits and studies I had made of her and hurled them to pieces on the floor. The shards of plaster flew against the windows and the ceiling. I snatched the drawings of her from the wall, tore them up and finished crushing them underfoot. And when I saw a piece of plaster that still had something to recognize her by I grabbed it again and smashed it to fragments on the floor. When everything had been destroyed I surveyed the ruins, dog-tired and panting. A great peace settled over me. It was as if I'd left everything behind me. As if I was absolutely empty. Then I saw the cat who had crept into the corner underneath a chair and was watching me with big frightened eyes. I pulled her out from under the chair, lay down on the bed and fell asleep, the cat on my chest.

The Witch's Headquarters

I spent the weeks that followed in bed, giving free rein to my lust for revenge in my imagination. I split their skulls with iron bars so their brains were sprayed around like snot, or I fired a heavy air-pistol against their temples, sabotaging their car and watching it crash and sink to the bottom of the Amsterdam-Rhine canal while they beat desperately on the windows and the wake of the ships erased all trace of the crime. I hauled their lifeless bodies along the beach and dragged them to a place where no one would find them. I had them squashed to pulp by a train at an unguarded crossing. I lynched them, broke them on the wheel, tortured them in cellars. I stamped them into the earth till nothing remained but the deep imprints of my heels. The only thing all these demoniacal day dreams proved to me was that I had lost her irrevocably. That I had lost. That all I could do when revenge, hate and anger ebbed away to a miserable, sickening longing for her was to jack off by her photos. And on my final gasping cry, the house of cards collapsing, I was left alone with myself and my soiled sheets. When I couldn't stand it any longer and fled that fetid lair, after first gathering the cat shit and the broken plaster, the putrid flowers that had collapsed down the side of the vase and were oozing on the table, the several feet of onion sprouts that were growing over the sink and the withered plants, and stuffing the lot in the dustbin, I went to Rotterdam. I had discovered his address and I don't think I meant to go there either to fight or to talk. I simply wanted to see the house he lived in. To look inside. To try and discover what it was. What attracted her to the man. Perhaps to get a glimpse of their happiness and love even. In a pub close by I waited until dusk. Then I walked into the street and found the number and looked to see if his name was on the door. I turned my face away as I walked past the lighted window, crossed the street, walked back and looked in from across the road. At first I thought I had the wrong house when I saw a woman and a child sitting at the table. I crossed and stood directly in front of the window. It was a woman in her thirties. A slovenly look about her. I felt a shock go through me. The little boy sitting beside her was an invalid. He was kind of mongoloid and his gestures were like those you see in health resorts. I felt sick. I wasn't capable of waiting at the tram stop. I hailed a taxi, let it drive me to the station and ducked into the first available train as if to try and escape the sadness of the whole affair. Some time in between my erotic debauches: "So with a grief like mine I should know what I'm doing," between Bella so and so who wanted to have her cunt licked with lapping noises before she gave herself and an Irene who wanted to bite you in the balls before you could nail her, I phoned Olga, my heart thumping. I got her mother on the phone who said she failed to see how I found the impudence to phone after everything I had done to her daughter. I said that her daughter was still my wife and if that had to come to an end then we should have to arrange one thing and another for a possible divorce. Then she gave me Olga. Her voice sounded dull. I asked, carefully, how things were. She said she still couldn't open her eye wide enough to see properly. I said that she had earned it. Then for a long time there was silence and I was afraid she would bang the receiver down. But she asked me why I'd phoned and if it wasn't finished between us. I said that was the most idiotic thing about it after so many years. It seemed impossible. That I wanted to talk to her. That she owed it to me and couldn't refuse. After a lot of pointless talk back and forth and reproaches on both sides she agreed. And so I found myself in the train to Alkmaar on that wet gangrenous day in May, riding through the dripping green landscape. I reflected that I should either take her back with me or else throttle her. And I did look like a strangler when I walked up their street. Sodden with rain and my hair in strands over my forehead and eyebrows. Before turning the corner I had lit a cigarette in a doorway even though it rained, so I looked a proper thug. Because pity is the greatest foe of love. They were standing by the window, Olga and her mother. She would have instructed her daughter thoroughly, that bitch. I could tell by looking at them. Now I also noticed the similarity in the way they looked at me. As if I were the prey. The black eye seemed to have gone. As I looked up and tried to pull a semblance of a smile around my rain-soaked cigarette, I thought: "Witch H.Q." That hailed back to Olga's father. When he took her to Amsterdam for the first time and they passed the tallest building with thick dark smoke belching out of its chimney, he had told her that the witches had their headquarters there. Just like he had said that the lame tobacconist was kept imprisoned in a cardboard box under the counter by his wife. When I sat across from her in the sitting room—her mother didn't show herself but I felt that she was under cover nearby, listening with her serpent ears pricked up and ready to burst in at the least flicker of trouble—we didn't really know what to say. She was wearing ready-made clothes that didn't suit her very much. That retained the imprint of the clothes hanger. I wondered what had happened to the striped dress. Maybe she'd put it in the dustbin, ashamed. Because she no longer felt like a polished apple in it. Anyway, it probably didn't fit her any more. She had grown thinner and I said so. Awkwardly, as with a first compliment. She said that a rolling stone gathers no moss. Then we were silent again. I stood up, walked to the window and looked at the blooming antirrhinums in the window sill; "Prick on a saucer," her father always called them. I looked across the street at the doorway where I had stood, years ago, to catch a glimpse of her. I reflected that after all this time I was as mad about her as I was then, and always would be. That it would never wear off. I clenched my fists because everything had now turned sour. Then, with my back towards her and my voice trembling, the recriminations came. She screamed back at me sometimes. With a hard, shrill note to her voice I'd never heard before. It grew into a full-scale quarrel that suddenly nauseated me because it was wrecking our last chance to get back together. I turned around and walked over to her. She backed away fearfully and I saw by her face that she wanted to call out "Mother" or "Mama." I reached her with a few strides and took her by the shoulders. She no longer dared to call out but looked anxiously at the door. I felt awful and tears welled up in my eyes because her one eye was still yellow and because she looked so afraid. Like a frightened animal that realises it can't escape. I loosened my grip and bent my face towards her. She drew back until her head bumped into the cupboard door. When I tried to kiss her she started to whisper hysterically: "This mouth has been kissed by someone else, you know. This mouth has been kissed by someone else." When I took her mouth in mine it stayed soft and weak and her body stayed limp as well. As if she would fall to the ground when I let her go. But she kept her teeth firmly clenched together. I couldn't reach her tongue. Then her mother coughed a few times from behind the door. "Tea anybody?", she asked with her faked voice. Yes, tea. So we sat down again, for hours, talking. About all the things you don't talk about. Because if you do they've already gone beyond repair. Talking has come too late, there's no point in it. Hours later, when my face was stiff from all that conversation and I felt my tongue sitting like something dry and unreal in my mouth, her mother rolled in a trolley with sandwiches but didn't show herself. I chewed through mine with distaste because it turned my stomach to eat bread that had been touched by that hag. Then we talked on. Or rather, I did. When I talked about her mother who was to blame for everything, putting ideas in Olga's head because she saw a profit for the firm in a marriage between her daughter and this man, I whispered and made accusing gestures at the door, as if all the evil that threatened us was behind it. At times she contradicted me, pale and doggedly. But mostly she listened and just shook her head if she didn't agree with something. A couple of times I hit below the belt by bringing her father into it. How much he had liked me and didn't care bugger all for this business about money because he could see she was happy. And that he would turn in his grave. It was out before I remembered that he and his ashes were in an urn. But I had to do it. I had to break her. I had to bore through that hard layer her mother wrought with her intrigue. After a silence I looked out of the window and I said I could still see her father standing there gazing up at the sky as he said: "I wish the sun would break through. But let's hope the two halves stay together." Or once coming back from Den Helder when he'd run into a rainstorm along the Noordholland canal: "It rained so hard the fish didn't know they were caught." Then the tears ran down her cheeks. It seemed as though her mother could smell the threat to her daughter because during the next attack, as Olga, eyes red from weeping, was about to give at the knees and had it on the tip of her tongue to say she was coming back with me, that viper knocked on the door and announced that it was time for me to go home, that it had taken long enough and was time for bed. When I looked at the clock it was too late to catch the train. That shrew would have simply put me out on the

108

street but after a whispered conference with Olga in the hall—even with my ear to the door I couldn't make it out—I was allowed to stay the night. Upstairs in the guest room. Olga's old room. It was still the same. It looked as if she had counted on her daughter to come back "under mother's wings" again. (It was still on the book shelf.) I hung my clothes over the little chair with the funny legs that Olga used to call the Frightened Deer chair and where she had sat in great suspense over Miss Headstrong's promise to cut off her braids at boarding school. I went in search of the place where she had cut into the curtains. Once she and her friend had held the fat girl from next door down on the bed and pulled her pants off. Just then her mother had come in with a plate of chocolates. Out of misgiving or shame for that fat naked bottom she had grabbed the scissors and snipped the curtain. Openly, so her mother saw it. She'd taken the thrashing of her life. I couldn't find it. The curtains must have been replaced or it had happened in the previous house by the canal. A house, she'd told me, where the water reflected on the ceiling and had been so restful that she'd spent hours lying flat on her back just looking at it. In the middle of the night I went to try Olga's bedroom door but it was locked, as I had suspected. I started knocking very softly but when I knocked louder I heard the light go on in her mother's bedroom. I quickly went to the can. Her father's notice was still glued to the inside of the door: DO YOU WANT A COLD SURPRISE? PULL THE CHAIN BEFORE YOU RISE! in his big awkward lettering. They must not have been able to get it off or it would have disappeared along with his snot chair. Since I guessed no one else had ever taken up his playful proposal I sat down when I pulled and went back to bed with a cold and damp behind. I couldn't sleep anyway. All her youth descended on me in that room with its play things of long ago: her books on the book shelf and her cuddly animals and little jugs and jars and other knick-knacks looking down on me from on top of the frame for the folding bed. But not one doll. Poor red animal. I saw her before me as the little girl I knew from photographs. With the broken front teeth that she couldn't hide because she always smiled at photographers. I heard the boys in her class shout: "Redlights!" and Pete Golhof say provocatively, as he tried to worm his hand between her clenched thighs: "Johnny's eleventh finger in Mary's second mouth." I saw her on this same bed playing Broken Prick with her girlfriends, remodelling the clay every time it broke from squirming around on top of one another. Here she sang with them: "One, two, three, four, five, six, seven, The teacher is giving a fucking lesson, In the middle of the gym, Filling all the maidens in, And those big boys, with their long toys, Teacher let me go again, Up and down is my refrain." I heard Nancy who had spent the Easter holidays with an aunt in the Amsterdam red light district whisper to her: "They leave with a red face. Then they stagger a bit on the steps. But I'm still going to find out what it's all about." And I saw her father as he lumbered into her room, heard him gasping for breath from the stairs and the walk in the park, as he said, excited as a child: "The black swan ate out of my hand." She had remembered because it was the day she first menstruated and she was cowering in her room because her mother wasn't home and she didn't know what to do. Several times I dropped into a kind of half-sleep from which I stirred mad with lust. I thought I was smelling her plum at a distance, like a dog. But I was afraid to go nosing around her door again. Because I knew that hell hound of a mother had her ears cocked. At times I created visions of terror inside my sleepy head. I heard the toilet flush, crept downstairs and grabbed when the tips of my fingers felt the soft cloth of her nightgown. Only when I had torn it to pieces in the struggle and was inside her did I feel that it was that horrible bitch. And she was the first thing to meet my eye when I looked outside in the morning, dizzy from the sleepless night. She was walking on the lawn with a head full of curling papers—the Medusa—her fattened dog behind her, protecting the mutt with a broomstick because she was in heat. I rushed downstairs and felt the door of Olga's bedroom. It was open. She was back sleeping like she used to, with her thumb in her mouth and her bum sticking out across the width of the bed. Quick as a flash I took off my underwear and slipped in beside her. I carefully pushed at her body until I had her in position. Her nightgown had worked itself up already from tossing and turning. It sat twisted about the upper part of her body like the drapery of a goddess in the Parthenon. Then I came down on top of her, softly pushed her thighs apart with my knees and pinned her to me. At first she stayed limp and heavy, but her thumb slipped out from between her sticky lips as they began to curl with appetite. But then she stiffened, even before opening her eyes. I threw my arms around her and pressed my mouth on her lips. Not so much to kiss her as to prevent her from crying out. While this double-backed animal wrestled without sense of direction, I kept thrusting savagely. When her mouth escaped me I thought she was going to scream. But she said that if I didn't get off her this instant and go, she would call her mother. It was such an idiotic thing to say that I laughed—

and almost slipped out of her. When I told her screaming wouldn't help since her mother was walking the
dog she decided to relax and let me have my way.
But she began to whisper, as urgently and hysterically
as the evening before, that someone else had had her.
And I began to yell at her, sobbing almost, that I
couldn't care less. That I loved her so desperately
that I could lick the seed of her lovers from her cunt.
And she almost came when I said that, she was letting herself go so bloody well. But I held back because
I wanted to leave her with something she wouldn't
forget in a hurry. Then she began to call out again,
for me to be careful. Especially now. As she wouldn't
even know who got her pregnant. But I kept thrusting and then she relaxed and let herself go altogether.
Just when we'd almost reached the climax there was a
violent banging on the door. Olga's whole body turned
to stone. Everything tensed and my prick was stuck
in her. Then her mother stormed in screeching, and
began to beat on the blankets as if she was performing an Oriental mourning rite, yelling that I was a
swine and a rapist and that she would call the police
if I didn't get out right now. Then she pulled the
blankets off us at the same time that my hard captured member ejected in Olga's stiffened body, to
the beat of my throbbing heart. And in spite of being
seized up with fright I heard Olga moan right by
my ear: "Aaahh." It seemed her mother could tell
by my clenched ass that I was putting a charge in
her daughter because she began to jerk and pull at
my ankles. And below me Olga renewed the struggle
by thumping me on the chest. I kicked myself free of
them, snatched up my underwear and walked out of
the room with the seed still dripping from my prick.
Before I slammed the door behind me I caught a
glimpse of Olga sitting in bed with her knees drawn

up and her arms thrown over her head as if she was expecting a beating. Even in the bathroom with the tap full on I could still hear the shrill bawling of that fishwife. But I felt triumphant and marvellous. Because she had gasped with pleasure under her mother's eyes. And when I had bathed, gloriously, in clouds of foam, and came out of the bathroom dressed and reborn, her mother was waiting for me in the corridor, pale with anger. I told her I was going to say goodbye to Olga and walked to the bedroom door. She tried to stop me. Her pale lips pressed together I shoved her aside but it didn't get me very far because Olga's door was locked again. I knocked, I pounded, called her name and finally shouted when she didn't reply. And that had kept calling to her daughter not to reply to such a swine. Then she went to the living room and stood in the doorway with the telephone in her hand threatening to phone the police if I didn't get out. I called out to Olga that I would phone her, that she was to come back to me. That she musn't let that bitch poison her. That I would always love her and wait for her. Then, without telling that pale crazed witch she was making a whore out of her daughter for the highest bidder or breathing any other fire or fury on her I left that house and I've never gone back there again.

Caesar and Brigitte Bardot

Man is treacherous. I pulled out all the stops. Gestures of despair when love no longer comes from both sides. When I saw her through the window of the bar where I was waiting for her, I quickly went over to the juke box and put on "How Much is That Doggie in the Window" which her father used to woof to all through the house. I'd played it already as I'd been an hour early bringing the marriage certificate, the deed of settlement and six hundred guilders in a buff envelope. Over the telephone we had arranged to bring three hundred guilders each for the solicitor, but I was certain that her mother would see to it that she hadn't a penny on her. I had read the deed at least twenty times. The dismal inventory of possessions "brought into the marriage" by the bride-to-be. An electric sewing machine (flogged to a girlfriend for next to nothing), divan with coverlet and other appurtenances (herself, I suppose), sundry forks, spoons and knives (brand Adolf H. or Gott mit uns). "The wife shall have jurisdiction over her personal and real property and the full enjoyment of the fruits. . ." She was off to a good start I thought as I watched her sail into the pub with a swish of the revolving door. She wore her hair loose. Combed out over her shoulders like a red screen. She was wearing a red suit with a white fur trim. Something from the winter sales. She must feel hot in it. When she spotted me she stalked over without looking left or right. Like a cat hunting something and blind to everything else. The men looked up from the reading table. They could tell by the clothes she wore. They gave her the up and down reserved for the female who can be persuaded. A provincial

114

bird out on the tiles. She stopped in front of my table. She didn't want coffee. We should go straight away. Oh, and she hadn't been able to get hold of three hundred guilders. So could I pay it for now. She hurried me out through the revolving door and I felt like jamming it with my foot and letting her plead, pound and yell in that glass cage until the waiters or the men at the reading table came to rescue her. She looked so ridiculous in that suit. As we were walking along the street I said that this was the first time I'd ever seen her in red. She said it was on everyone's lips in Alkmaar: "Have you seen Olga yet?" And that she'd worn brown for quite a while. When I reminded her that she'd only been gone from me a few months she started to laugh and said that she had all kinds of periods, just like Picasso. And when I asked her about the striped dress she told me she'd given it to the maid. Who was ecstatic with it. But who'd had to take it in so it would fit her. On the steps of the solicitor's office I had my first chance to have a good look at her she had been walking so fast and I saw why she looked so chalky and strange and seemed to have lost her identity. It wasn't just the clothes. It was her face. I missed her freckles. Only then did I see that her beautiful rosy skin with its little brown specks was covered with a thick layer of brownish pancake that carelessly stopped at her neck so the skin below looked blue and sickly. I wanted to say something as it made me want to cry. But I restrained myself because what did it have to do with me, anyway. She had jurisdiction over her personal and real property now. She could even stick her head in pancake batter or walk around in her mother's grey pleated skirts if she wanted to. She looked at me and saw the tears in my eyes. She didn't know, of course, that they were from helpless rage. From the pancake, that white rabbit fur, all the rest of the crap. So she said just before the door opened: "It has to be done, love. It has to be done." The jellyfish of a solicitor led us to his office in person. A soft greasy colossus with a stomach like a beerbarrel, his belt keeping the staves together. A very noticeable mouth, pink and wet with spit, sat in his huge beard, a beard with scabs of dandruff in it. I knew him from the city. A noted art café visitor. He made me hand over the six hundred guilders and then pressed a Saxon shepherd and shepherdess in my hands and asked me—in my capacity as sculptor I suppose— what they were worth since he wanted to sell them. I looked at his hole-in-the-wall china vaguely and put it back on the mantle-piece, saying that the honorarium for my consultations came a good bit higher than his. He swallowed the offence by laughing heartily, his stomach splashing about and then wetted his enormous thumb by pressing it to his lips and damped his way through a bunch of papers from which he gabbled something now and then. I only half-listened and looked at the wall lined with lawbooks, a student annual from the year zero and a deluxe edition of the *Decameron*. I threw a quick look at Olga when I heard that bloated pig grunt: "A demand for divorce on the grounds of adultery committed by her". She was staring at the ceiling as if it was of no importance to her. As if she was in the doctor's waiting room, forced to listen to the confidences of other patients. She picked some bits of rabbit fluff off her red skirt and then I noticed that her nails were as long as shells and varnished pink. And I caught myself with the reaction: "Nice little claws around your prick", not associating her with them at all. The meatpudding in front of us had finished, settled his gut comfortably between

116

his legs like a Japanese monk and said, looking at us in turn: "Caesar and Brigitte Bardot. What a pity. I wonder if I could manage to bring the turtledoves back together." He knew that it couldn't be done. That he could safely let the six hundred marbles bulge from his wallet. But out of revenge for that bit of rural porcelain he slipped Olga a piece of paper for me to sign before the divorce, if she could get me to do it. It was something to the effect that I declared she hadn't really committed adultery and it had just been the means of getting the divorce. He added that she, as a divorcee, would not be allowed into certain countries without that paper. South Africa for instance. I remarked that the more criminal and murderous the country, the more hypocritical it was in sexual matters and that he surely wasn't suggesting we would go to a country where they treated ninety percent of the population like animals. He observed with a fine irony that the lady would be deciding these matters for herself in future and that was the end of the transaction and we were back on the street. She wanted to be on her way but then remembered the paper I still had to sign and accepted my invitation to have a drink somewhere. I hailed a taxi and we drove to the Vondel Park. As we strolled along the wide avenues leading to the Rotunda, the shrubs bursting into flower, she flirted openly with every passing man taking his dog or himself for a walk. To taunt me I'm sure and to show that she was free to do as she pleased. To show how she'd had to restrain herself in the past and was now making up for lost time. I didn't care. It was better that she tried to hurt me than to have her sorry for me. Pancake seemed to draw them more than freckles. Our walk had elements of the cartoon where the girl enters the doctor's office, a throng of men behind her and says: "Doctor, I have a bit of dirt in my eye." It didn't matter, as once we sat on the terrace hidden by a hedge the flirting stopped. But she jumped up impatiently again and said she had to make a phone call. On her return she told me that she couldn't stay very long as she was going to be picked up at the main entrance in half an hour. I asked her if that's why she had the crud on her face and she bit back at me that she'd put it on because she looked so pooped. She said she'd stay long enough for a Campari, but I had our usual gin and cola. Sipping at her bitter drink she produced the paper, put it in front of me on the table and asked me to sign it. All very casually. I bent over it and pretended to read with great attention for at least five minutes before she asked me if I hadn't finished reading it yet. When I told her I didn't see why I should sign it since she bloody well did commit adultery, she said that had nothing to do with it. That wasn't the point. I felt like taking her by the throat and squeezing. Pushing that powder-puffed face into her glass and bawling what the hell was it about if not her goddamned adultery. But I quietly stayed where I was and looked at the gravel between my feet. She picked the paper up and said: "Don't then." Suddenly it struck me as all so damned pathetic and that I was pissed off with the whole thing. I took the paper out of her hands, borrowed her fountain pen and wrote: WHATEVER YOU HAVE DONE, WHAT-EVER YOU DO OR WILL DO, WHEREVER YOU GO, I WILL ALWAYS LOVE YOU! And signed. I gave it back to her and she read it. She screwed it up into a ball which she put in her handbag and said: "Now it's worthless." Then she stood up and without saying goodbye she walked away past the tables and out through the exit.

Smorgasbord

After living through hell it was a long slow road getting back to work. I didn't make mothers and children or Persephones any more. In the junk dumped along the Amstel I ferretted out rusty wire from garden gates and chicken coops, broken toys, old kitchen utensils, bits of rock and cork and arranged all this on wooden boards back in my studio, glued the whole lot into place, poured tar over it and gold-varnish, or speckled it with plastic crystals. Then I'd go over it with the oxy-acetylene torch. Until the seething mass boiling under the thick black skin clotted to a piece of scorched earth. And I'd have another painting. Sometimes I'd make two or three of these in a day. Until my studio was lined with them and began to look like a bat cave. Paintings that, by their weight alone scared the art lovers. And when I got tired of it all and I could have puked just from the smell of those carcasses I stacked a load of them in my old Riley (the pram had gone through its springs while Olga was still with me, giving up the ghost under the weight of my brain-children) and drowned them in the Amstel as of yore, but this time by myself and in the middle of the night. Olga once said when the ducks were diving there: "They're going to the exhibition." The fanatical energy I threw into my work, my scorched and tattered appearance and the dustbin-look with which I sought out refuse apparently made me look like a foreign tramp, as during Cancer Week a peppery female who was rattling a collection box on the Damrak changed the language of her appeal to English when she saw me coming: "Cancer...

Cancer...!" And once, when I came out of a pub where I'd had a cup of coffee, an old lady hissed at me: "Liquor is poison." I no longer took girls home. The last two had been a pain in the arse. I had resolved to put a stop to it. No more buggering around in my house. You're better off going to the whores. Cheaper, too. You don't have to pour drinks down them and you don't have to spend hours listening to all kinds of bullshit. Half an hour and you're out on the street again, ready to go back to work. And yet it had begun pleasantly enough with Swedish Astrid. I had momentary reservations when she left such forcefully crushed butts in the ashtray. But I threw caution to the winds in the face of that magnificent piece of softness from Sweden, that perfect pin-up. The first evening it all seemed so beautiful. It crossed my mind that she could be a second Olga. I told her I would write a declaration of love on her stomach in Swedish. And I took her cherry-red lipstick to that lovely blond shield that seemed as if it would lift off if you put your thumb in the hollow and wrote: SMORGASBORD She didn't think it was funny, but how in hell should I have known what "I love you" was in Swedish. In the beginning she was sweetness itself. Loving and tender. But gradually she began to find more and more fault. She meant to build herself a little nest. It wasn't enough that I showered in the mornings, she wanted me in there before we went to bed as well. Or she might buy me a health toothbrush, the kind with a hairy knob at the end so you gag on a mouthful of bristles. One day it was the sheets; they had become soiled again. They were to be changed that instant and she began to pull them off. When I said no she turned into an icicle and lay stiff and cold beside the pile of sheets. A few days later when she left the bed to go to the can the number of cat fleas jumping on her legs made her look as though she'd pulled on net stockings. She cursed and screamed at me in her Uddevalla English as I trampled the sheets laughing. She rubbed her legs and plucked them clean, pulled her tasteful clothes over her neat body and disappeared from my life. Thea, one of the last flowers to bloom from my bedclothes, went even quicker. At the end of a fucking session when she was sitting on the edge of my bed with a banana in her hand (she had cut it in half and was spooning the fruit out like a soft-boiled egg) she told me that after they announced Marilyn Monroe's death over the radio she'd cried for an hour. I sat up, and my heart missed a beat. When I'd heard that same announcement it had been as if Olga had died. As if, with that news item, Olga too had gone forever. To hide my confusion I said that I probably couldn't even do a mock-up of Marilyn without getting an erection. (But stiff back or stiff knees, You stand straight at Tiffany's.) She jumped as if she'd been sitting on a scorpion and began to slap me uncontrolledly. I let her have her rage at first, but when she gave me a clout on the nosebone that almost knocked me out cold, I suddenly saw red, dragged her from the bed and bundled her out of the door, naked, throwing her clothes after her into the windy night. From then on it was all over. They were staying out. That same night I took the box with all the hairpins, earrings and brooches found under and behind my bed in the course of time, and emptied it in the dustbin. The only thing I saved was an earring in the shape of a sea-horse that Ans or Wies or Riekie used to fix onto on my cock when we were frolicking on the bed. From then on I went into the city when I needed a woman, until I found one who was not only conge-

nial but had her own house or room as well. And
so it was that I found myself in the Appollo-Laan,
in a house stowed full of shiny, expensive kitsch,
where you could roll from loft to cellar on the fur
and velvet floor in your mothernaked without once
grazing yourself; lying in bed with a woman so elegant, a sailing ship of more mast than stern, that
I heard myself ask after doing her over: "Did you
come, Madam?" And after a while I knew the city's
highest peaks: girls' rooms up stairs so steep and
twisting that you needed the dexterity of a mountain
goat as well as its lewdness to reach your goal.
Rooms split off the front or back end of the attic
with some slipshod boards. Where you had to thread
your way in the pitch dark through the washing
of the downstairs neighbours on your way to the
seams of light coming through the partition. The
usual reproductions of a sepia drawing of a Moroccan
dancer by Delacroix, an opera scene by Toulouse
Lautrec or some Degas ballerinas on the wall. I can
still hear some of their voices say the things I particularly remember: "Turn around for a change",
"Shall we insert small objects into each other?" "Their
tools look ten years older than they do." Gertie,
mad as a leek, had pasted shells all over one wall
of her attic room and when she asked me to give her
a couple of good swishing cracks on the behind with
a riding crop, she'd press her bare front into those
sharp-edged shells, calling: "Flog me, master! Flog
me!" She used to work in an institution, in charge
of speechless beings who did nothing but lie there
excreting muck and slime, and who were referred
to as "seedlings". Later she had taken a course that
enabled her to teach mongoloid children. A paper-
over her desk bore the words: MONGOLISM
IS ONE CHROMOSOME TOO MANY like a

proverb. And underneath in her almost illegible hand: *Mongolism is therefore not caused by alcoholism, venereal disease or having a child late in life. It is a fault in meiosis.* You had to be very sadistic with those chubby little things sometimes, she said; out of guilt their parents spoiled them so much that they were often too lazy to take off their own coats. If that was the case she'd pick them up and sit them on top of the cupboard all morning. But soon after they'd become very attached to her again. As she arrived in the morning they would storm up to her in the corridor in great excitement and somersault around with joy. From there my diaspora led back to that dismal backroom in Amsterdam West with a view of verandas full of washing, zinc wash tubs and Vespas covered over with plastic. To that divorced girl with her three snot-bubbling toddlers. When I came in bearing sweets for the children, who called me uncle, she immediately shepherded me into a ramshackle cane chair as though I should amass all my energies before we landed in the bedroom. And turning on the radio she'd say: "You stay in your nice easy chair with a little music and Ina will bring you a bracing cup of soup." And then I spent the next few hours with the small fry on my lap telling stories until their wet little bottoms had soaked the legs of my trousers. When I helped her with the dishes and she went for a dry tea towel she said: "Just a minute love, Ina will give you a thirsty teatowel." The gloomy feeling that it couldn't last long. That their second father would fade away too. And I was gone from home for such long spells that the water in the reservoir was rusty when I pulled the chain like after a holiday and the cat sniffed everything in the house as if she was with strangers when I brought her home from the neighbours. The scenes kept on changing.

123

Other meetings, other children, other rooms. That first Christmas without Olga, when the melancholy of being alone would have killed me, found me struggling with a dead rabbit in the Pijp. In the courtyard of a miserable ground-floor flat where a little Surinam mother lived with her dream of a six-year old daughter. The black knight had left them in the lurch. In a reckless moment I'd said I could prepare the beast the Surinam way just as well as her husband and then I was in for it. It wasn't to be skinned but shorn (and without breaking the skin) and then air was to be pumped between the skin and the meat with a bicycle pump. It then went into the oven with everything still in and on. I just couldn't accept that the guts weren't coming out first. But she insisted on it being done this way as otherwise you couldn't keep the air in. But it didn't get as far as that. Standing there among the tufts of fur with her husband's razor in my frozen hands (it wouldn't have surprised me in the least if one of the neighbours spying from behind their illuminated, perforated Christmas stars had telephoned the RSPCA) I suddenly couldn't do it. When I thought that this half-bald blue-grey brute that closely resembled a deformed still-born baby was yet to be pumped up, my gorge rose. I'd had enough. I searched out the kitchen knife, skinned the rabbit, cut him open, pulled out the insides and hacked him to pieces in the time-honoured manner. She was disappointed, my black princess. Late that evening as we rigged the little Christmas tree for her daughter she was very quiet. But when she was lying against me in bed she said that it didn't matter all that much, that the rabbit would taste just as nice the Dutch way tomorrow. I looked across her shoulder through the fly-specked curtains and there, in the shine of the streetlight, I saw the first snowfall of the year. And I told her I had a surprise in store for Christmas morning. When she asked me what it was I didn't want to tell her, but then I told her anyway: "A white Christmas." She turned around and we watched together as the snow fell. And she began to hum "I'm dreaming of a white Christmas." And I sang along with her damn it. Because if you can't get that sick, trashy Bing Crosby slobber across your lips in the shabby dirt and gloom of the Pijp when you've come through a year of shit and un- happiness like mine, you might as well write yourself off.

The Cursing Nails

With the new year the father and mother game abruptly stopped. I could no longer stay away from home for nights on end. I had become a father myself. By accident. Even if it was only of a black-headed gull. I was at work in my studio, my sleeves rolled up and to my elbows in sludge, when I suddenly heard a car screech to a halt. Going outside I found a little van by my door. The driver was standing in front, a gull lying at his feet. He said he couldn't figure it out. He hadn't even touched the bird. It had been on the road picking away at a squashed piece of bread and he'd jammed on the brakes because it hadn't had the sense to get out of the way in time. It had flapped up past his windscreen and then fallen down. He carefully stirred the white body with his foot and said he imagined the thing was dead. Probably died of fright. I told him I would take it into the house in case there was a recovery, quickly went back in to rinse off my arms and returned with a box, laid the gull in it and brought it inside. It was a black-headed gull. His bill and feet were a beautiful bright red and there were a few chocolate-coloured spots by his eye. But I didn't have time to fuss around with him because the bucketful of mush I was slapping on a wooden board would soon be too hard to work with. As I was working away, I suddenly had the feeling I was being watched. I looked up to find the gull staring at me, his head over the edge of the box. Curious, no doubt, as this must be the first time in his life he'd witnessed the making of a painting. When I was finished I walked over to the box. He ducked back into his feathers. I carefully felt the wings but it didn't seem as if anything was broken so I tossed him lightly up in the air. But he fell fluttering at my feet and stayed there, on his side, with his wings spread out. As I picked him up he left his first signature on the floor. I put the box in the car and drove to the vet, the same one who had operated on my cat in the middle of the night. He remembered it, he said, while examining the gull and not finding anything to prevent it from flying. There had been a thunderstorm, he remembered that as well. He asked me if we'd been able to keep the kittens alive. I said that they had received tender loving care. That she had breastfed them with lukewarm milk from a Maggi bottle. In his opinion the gull would fly again in a few days, that the bird was obviously mixed up just now. As I departed with my box, he told me to give his best regards to my wife. I nodded and knew it was that kiss of heartfelt gratitude that Olga had given him. Something you'd never forget. At home I put the gull in the sitting room. There was nothing there anyway and I didn't think he would take exception to the motto left by the American birds HE WHO PUTS SALT IN THE SUGAR BOWL IS A MISANTHROPE which had remained on the wall, almost illegible on the yellowed paper. It occurred to me to change it to "He who puts a seagull in the sugar bowl is a misanthrope", but no one came round now and for myself the thought above was enough. I filled the dish pan with water and put it in the middle of the room. A few times a day I went in to feed him chopped fish. At first he didn't want to eat it from my hand, but when he was hungry enough he plucked it off my outstretched fingers. And I chased him every once in a while to see if, in order to escape, he would take wing. But no, he just ran away from me, his feet clattering on the linoleum which soon turned into an encrusted, stinking, white-brown field. I even put pieces of board under him to create a new kind of painting: Imprints of gull's feet in living shit, but no one thanked me for them. Animal lovers are seldom art lovers. And you'd need an underdeveloped olfactory organ because those paintings stank like a chicken coop in a fishmonger's. Coming home at night I'd find him standing on one red leg in the middle of the dishpan when I switched on the light in his room. And it made me realize how difficult I'd find it to give him his freedom should he ever decide to fly again. During the first part of that year (I should call it the Year of the Gull, as he stayed eight months and I grew terribly fond of him—even my cat couldn't resent that sweet bird for long) only the vaguest of news about Olga reached me. A few months after the divorce she'd wanted to rush headlong into marriage in Scotland. But she had abandoned the plan at the last minute and decided to wait out the appointed nine months. However her mother wished to make her presence felt once more before leaving the sinking ship. Venomous as ever. She sent me an account. Via her solicitor. She wanted to bloody well have me pay for the linoleum she'd given to Olga for her birthday two years ago. The shabby shit colour Olga used to stand on in her kitchen that had changed to a brilliant Mediterranean blue overnight. All the same it hadn't taken her long to pit the new linoleum with her high heels, and in some places it was completely perforated. I was supposed to pay for this? I was off to a solicitor before the dust settled. Not to that foul corrupted toad of the divorce. No, this time I happened on a decent man who sent a polite but crushing reply to her solicitor: *My client informs me that your client effected the purchase of material and labour as itemized in the account you refer to out of generosity towards her daughter and my client, and that there is not the slightest question that this account could have been paid under the heading of loan to my client. Said client therefore sees no cause to observe any payment to your client.* She could stuff that in her pipe and smoke it. And smoke it she did because I heard no more. In the autumn of the Year of the Gull (I eventually had him jumping on my lap when I brought fish), I saw Olga in the Bijenkorf. I was carting a Congolese nail sculpture along like a fakir rather than leave it in my car, because none of the doors on this vehicle would lock. I had just exchanged it with a friend for a painting of similar weight. The body of the sculpture was as full of rusty nails as a porcupine and there was a mirror in the stomach giving the impression of built-in television. Suddenly I noticed Olga rummaging in a tray of gloves. Men's gloves it shot through me, before I decided that this couldn't be Olga because it was a blonde. I watched her for quite a while before I went over to stand behind her and said: "At home I still have an envelope with some of your red hair." She turned round as if I'd pinched her bottom. I'd confused her and she blushed. But then she tightened her face and looked at me without expression as if I was someone in the crowd. I recalled what I had been told not so very long ago: "The warmth has gone from her eyes." I could see it was true but I refused to believe it. I managed to get her into the lift up to the coffee-bar and resolved not to mention that red hair again. There we were, with a view of the city and the statue in front of us between the cups. I felt overwhelmed by sadness because at first there wasn't a trace of what had been. As if I had simply embarked on my latest adventure. As if in an hour or so I would be left with the after-taste of a quickie in my mouth. And I couldn't bear to think like that where Olga was concerned. The Olga that was. I asked her who she was buying gloves for and she said: "I was just looking." Then she asked me what the thing with the nails was and didn't stub out her cigarette but lit another from it. I said that the mirror was the seat of a spirit. And that the nails were cursing nails: you belted them in when you wanted to harm an enemy. Without smiling she said that I must have hammered a good many in there for her. I laughed and told her it had been quite bare when I brought it into the Bijenkorf but that when I saw her standing there I had promptly rammed it full of nails. When I looked at her she looked away. It was the hair. I could hardly stand to look at it. How could she have done it? The fool. She looked as though the blight had got

129

her. Pathetic. But phoney, too. Like a photograph that's been coloured in. When I talked of the gull covering the sitting room floor with an ever thickening layer of dirt, she suddenly began to talk about her mother. Probably because she was ashamed of that account for the linoleum. She said that her mother was really very nice. That her mother's house was always open to her when the need arose. But that she took too much money out of the firm at a time when business was slack, and insisted nevertheless on going to Austria with her girlfriend every year, fully equipped as The Merry Widow of the ski slopes. And she kept having difficulties with the staff. After a towel disappeared from the lavatory she had refused to hang another in its place unless the stolen one was returned. She had stuck a note under the hook that said: THAT WHICH HUNG HERE WAS STOLEN ON THE 26TH OF MAY! When I asked Olga how she herself was doing and was she still so sweet, she said with a bitchy look: "Can't you tell? Doesn't the passion shine from my eyes?" But a little while later she was telling me, somewhat despondently, about that first peccadillo. It had been brief because the man was a weakling. His wife was English. Marriage to a foreigner had fascinated him at first and he tried to speak the kind of anglicized Dutch that people who have emigrated fall into after a couple of years abroad. But he didn't have the guts to get a divorce because his father had threatened to disinherit him if he did. He was impotent with fear of that man. He kept crying on her shoulder for his little crippled boy who couldn't be left to his fate either. She said that he was so sorry for himself that while they were at an inn in Kijkduin he had tried to commit suicide in her presence. With sleeping pills. While studying his reactions in the mirror over the wash-basin. It had all been for show but being so wrapped up in his own face he had accidentally taken too many. She'd had to phone for an ambulance to take him away. They had pumped out his stomach at the hospital. When on top of everything else his father had phoned to tell her it was time to call it a day, that his son staged three or four of these odious scenes a year, she'd had enough. She hadn't even gone to see him in the hospital. Her mother was furious. Not only had she lost an important client, she was left with Olga to support. When I asked her why she hadn't come back to me after it was over she said: "I couldn't. All I wanted was a quiet life to feel at peace. And nothing more. A bit of going out and sitting at bars. To be with strangers." I told her that when I heard she had remarried I had always imagined it was to that man. She shook her head and said that after all this wretched business she couldn't have borne it to have him breathing down her neck. She was married to a business connection in Alkmaar. A man who was only interested in soccer and Churchill. He was very well up in both. When I asked her if her mother had been behind that lot too she suddenly snarled at me: "You always think everything is my mother's fault. He has been coming to our house for years." We didn't speak for a while and her fingers fiddled at the nails of the sculpture. She said the mirror would be quite useful for doing your make-up in. Suddenly I asked her if she was happy. She nodded, and then I saw a bit of the old Olga when she told me she had a little green turtle in an aquarium with a piece of treebark and that she'd love to have a turtle that could disappear completely in his shell like the one we'd seen in the Zoo. A box turtle. And that she wanted a baby goat in the spring. I asked her jokingly if she'd seen an empty swimming pool yet because I remembered her saying, walking past the Miranda Pool long ago: "I have a deep desire to see a swimming pool without water." I told her that I had walked in there last winter when the door was open. That they gave you a strange sinking feeling, those big tanks of blue-green tile with dry leaves heaped in the corners and all those empty dressing cubicles. The deserted play meadow had looked friendlier and had reminded me of summer. As if the spectres of those plump seals in the neighbourhood who went there "for a quick dip" at seven o'clock in the morning as part of their awkward weight-reducing exercises haunted the place. She also remembered being stung by a wasp in the middle of winter. In the snow of the Amsterdam Wood. She had forgotten her gloves and folded down the cuffs of her coat. Where the wasp was spending the winter. Then she closed up. She didn't allow herself to talk any more about that time two years ago, a past that seemed so terribly far away. It didn't suit her in any case, the way she looked, the way she was. But I still couldn't suppress a feeling of triumph and I thought: "You'll be back for more." But first she'd have to take a few more knocks from life. She walked back with me to my car and loved it on sight. She asked me if I remembered the time when I'd been given an advance on a commission and we'd gone after an advertisement for an old 1946 Jaguar. I added how insulted the garage proprietor had been that we expected the thing to be in running order for seven hundred guilders. She laughed and sat down in my place behind the wheel a moment. She pushed in the accelerator and the brake and the clutch. I looked at her moving legs and was reminded of that first time I met her. When she gave me a lift. She got out and said that these were hardly the clothes for such a car. That it was a car for slacks and a jumper. But that those days were gone. She had to be a lady now. As I was guiding in the nail sculpture at the other side of the car, she ducked her head in and looked at a painting of mine standing up in the back. She asked me if that was what I was doing nowadays and if I still managed to get rid of them. I said that I often sold them. To newly-wed intellectuals in those modern flats in the suburbs. Because they were very effective sound-proofing. But that I often chucked carloads of them into the Amstel. Like we used to with the pram. She shrugged her shoulders and said she must be on her way. She offered me a hand and I shook it freely and naturally because not for a moment had I expected we would kiss goodbye. She said that we'd probably run into each other again. Then she disappeared in the crowd. For some weeks following that meeting I felt like hell. Hearing her story of that first affair took away the foundation of the agony I'd gone through at the time. It made a snot and tears melodrama of the whole business. I went back to my gull for comfort. Not like animal lovers do when they whisper their hate of mankind into furry ears or teach their parrot to swear. But for peace. It was like being at the Diorama in the Zoo as I sat there on the old chair with the seaweed stuffing coming out, looking at my gull standing stock-still on the shit-covered boards as if it was on a sand bank. Or with his red feet paddling furiously around in the dish pan while his wings splashed large pearls of water over himself. When I came in one morning he suddenly flew up and began to fly around me with wide strong wing-beats. It was as if the space smashed to pieces. His wing tips seemed to push the walls of the little room out. He kept on flying around

133

me. And then I broke down. I stood there and sobbed out the whole dirty, filthy, stinking mess of those last two years. And with my face taut from crying I put him in a box and drove him to the dike along the Amstel. There, by the sandy waste, with the gulls over the pools of water in the distance, I opened the box. He flew up to the sky at once. And, as is fitting to the farewell of a bird, circled over my head a few times. Then he was taken up into a whole flight of shrieking and screeching gulls. I would have called, cried out, but I couldn't produce a single sound. It seemed as though someone behind me had locked his hands around my neck and was squeezing my throat with all the strength in his fingers.

Nice Dolls and Judas Dolls

I was on my knees for days scraping the crust of bird shit off the floor. In the end I met with success but the room remained uninhabitable. The stench, a racy melange of bird shit and dried flounder, could be cut with a knife. It seemed as though the walls exhaled it, but it came from the softened muck that had run under the skirting together with the scrubbing water. I tried everything. Scattering soap powder, sprinkling Eau de Cologne, leaving a dish filled with turpentine. It didn't help. For a few days it might reek of the other stink, but then that all-permeating stench drifted out of the cracks and joints again.

I couldn't let the room any more. All it was good for was a junk room, just like in Olga's time. So my loneliness became complete once more. I had neither gull nor girl. I kept to myself. I worked and I slept. After that last meeting with Olga something in me seemed to have snapped. All the illusions and the hope that had sustained me through the months of misery were gone. And where others take to drink or dope I drugged myself with work. From early in the morning till late at night. A year passed before I had news of her again. Via a girl we both knew and who was still in contact with Olga. A month after we met in the Bijenkorf Olga had come to this girl for the address of a helpful doctor. She had become pregnant, and it finished the second marriage. She couldn't bear to have that man around her now she'd said. She locked herself in the bedroom at night and he drowned the marital crisis at the local bar. He came home drunk every night and toppled on the divan in the sitting room to sleep. But when he turned aggressive and smashed all the furniture one night, kicked in the bedroom door and, breathing beer-fumes all over her, tried to rape her, she grabbed a suitcase of clothes and fled to her mother once again. And since the friend's doctor had run into the law while doing his abortions, she had the child taken away by a needlewoman with soap suds. It left her with infected ovaries and one of them had to come out after a little while because you knew her by the stench of her cunt. Now she was just about to marry again. An American engineer who was with an oil company. The friend had mentioned they were going to the America immediately after the wedding and since I would perhaps never see her again, I wrote her a note. After a few days she phoned me, from Beverwijk, where she and her future husband

135

had rented a house with some other American couples who worked for the same company. We made a date for the following day and in the hours before she arrived I walked up and down my studio like a tiger before feeding time. I tried to see everything with her eyes. If this or that had been there when she still lived with me. And suddenly there she was, in person. She looked around her as I had done just before. I wondered what was going on inside her. Did she see the cactuses were gone, and all the plaster portraits for which she'd posed so many hours while listening to Sonny Rollins or Miles Davis records. She stood a long time by the sculpture of her and the cat. Then she asked where the cat was. The cat was lying on a chair asleep and hadn't reacted to Olga's voice. It was too long ago. Olga didn't move, just looked somewhat timidly in her direction. Maybe she was rather glad the animal slept on. It would have been a strange sight in any case if she had taken the cat in her arms. She sat down and I put a bottle of brandy and glasses on the table. She shocked me when she came in. She'd grown so thin and looked nervous and ill. Her hair was red again and very short. She said it had to be cut to get rid of the blond. In the beginning she'd looked like a bleached poodle. But it was essential, as she had dyed it blonde for her last husband and hated any reminder of him. She poured herself a drink and said the studio was exactly as it used to be. Except for the paintings. She hadn't missed the cactuses. Or her portraits. Perhaps she'd already forgotten all about them. I just sat looking at her. This made her restless and ill at ease and she asked me if I thought she'd grown old. I mustered a smile and said that she'd grown older but not old. But I could have wept for the loss of that beautiful girl of mine. And then as she drank her brandy out came the tale of her second marriage. She had been half out of her wits with fear of getting pregnant all those months, because he didn't want to take any precautions. He was coarse and stupid. There'd been nothing of any value between them. With him she'd had the feeling of living in a large rabbit hutch. Nothing but straw and her own turds. She couldn't even remember what he looked like. She had totally forgotten him. I asked her if she thought about me like that but she said that if that was the case she wouldn't be here. Then she got up and walked over to the tree trunk still standing in the centre of my studio and asked if I remembered that it had come out of their garden. I said that her mother had it chopped down a month after her father's death because it made the house so gloomy. Her father had never wanted it done. She recalled that small branches with tender green leaves had come out of the bark here and there when we first had it. As though the tree wanted to express the last bit of life in itself. But the leaves soon withered because the tree could no longer pull food and moisture from the earth. And she still knew that when the trunk had just been put there, an enormous stream of red ants had come out of it, running right across the studio and disappearing through a crack in the floor. It had taken the whole day before they were all gone and I hadn't let her sprinkle any poison. I said that those ants had had the colour of her hair and that's why I wouldn't allow it. But at the time I'd had the feeling they were travelling back underneath the ground to her father. To the garden where they belonged and where they'd always lived. She sat down again and when she asked me for the photos we had taken because she was curious how she used to look, I put the whole box of them in front of her

137

on the table. She looked at it without moving for a moment, her glass in her hand. Then she took them out one by one, almost reluctantly, and studied them long and hard. Those early photos, when she still had that naughty look. With the pink hat and the lovely full mouth and the jumper pulled down around her naked shoulders, the black and white striped jumper that I burnt later on. As a gypsy, in her long flowered nightie leaning up against the mottled grey linen of our tenthouse behind the dunes with that swing in her hips and her face still puffed with sleep. And I wondered if she remembered sleeping behind that dirty linen with the little mountain duck between her lovely tits and how happy we had been there, in that whitewashed wooden bed. In working clothes with a scarf around her head and covered with white spatters from helping me pour the plaster. Dancing in the sea, all cuddles and curves, with a fishing boat showing through the sprays of water. With the puss on her arm changing from kitten to cat. On the balcony, skinning the pickling onions. And later, proudly in front of the shelf, the glass jars filled with vinegar and red peppers and bay leaves clearly visible between the white globes. I looked at her intently as she jumped from landmark to landmark. I saw her face wanting to push back emotions. She'd say to herself: "That's when I wore the purple dress." "That was by the blackthorn. On the corner. We picked them in the dark with the flashlight. I'd forgotten that too." Coming to the nude photos of herself she was actually ashamed. She wasn't even aware how often I had jacked off by them, trying like mad to raise that fair flesh of hers out of the grey picture. I said that the one before the mirror had been taken after she fingered herself in front of me. That you could still tell by the curl of her lips. She acted as though she hadn't heard me and went on looking. But suddenly she said that her present figure gave her an inferiority complex. That her breasts weren't what they used to be when everyone said: "Olga has the best ones." And that she put pancake on her legs at the beach to cover up the varicose veins. She never undressed in the daylight now and wore long sleeves because she didn't like the freckles on her arms any more. When I said I should still like to kiss them, one by one, she said that I persisted in seeing her as she used to be. That I idealized her when she had stopped being the ideal woman a long time ago. The man she was going to marry loved her as she was. It didn't matter to him if she was drunk and spoiled the bidding at bridge showing off how smart she was or completely changed her hair style. When I asked her what kind of a man he was, she said I would think he had a terribly interesting face. He was terribly ugly. Not in features so much, but in that it was a pock-marked face. An Indian face. He looked like Humphrey Bogart she said. And he worshipped the ground she walked on in a manner of speaking. When I said that I'd worshipped her too she nodded in agreement but started on a stream of reproaches. How locked up she'd been, not going into the city by herself even once in all those years. That I took her to bed much too often. Beginning in the morning when she might be in the kitchen making our first cup of coffee. She'd think. "Here we go again." She had worked it out, as much as seven times some days. That couldn't be called normal. I had satyriasis. When she asked if it was still that way with me I said that if she had stayed it would have been. When I asked her if she couldn't laugh about the things we used to do she said: "No, I've stopped laughing.

When I started out I thought, life is a fairy tale. I shall marry, I will be happy. But I am a lot less happy than I thought I would be." She looked silently at the photo in her hand a while, the one where she pressed the mountain duck to her cheek. She looked so lovely and happy in it. Like the rose that grows in the dunes. I saw her swallow and told her to put all the photos she wanted aside. I'd have prints made for her. But she shook her head and put the photo back in the box, face down. Then she pushed it away from her to the centre of the table and said, as she rose, that she would come back to sort them out another time but that she must go now as she still had to buy a bottle of brandy for bridge that evening, and it was almost six o'clock already. She promised to come once more before she left for America. At the door I suddenly captured her and kissed her on both cheeks. Because I thought I would never see her again. And the tears almost ran down my face. But she did come. A week later. With her husband of two days. He really did look like Humphrey Bogart and I could see that she'd been right in what she said. He did worship the ground she walked on. He looked at her in just the same way as I had done all those years. At last she was someone's treasure again and it nearly made me happy too. But he also was afraid he might lose her. As I had been. Because when she stood up from the low bench where she was sitting with him to go to the lavatory, he threw his arms around her legs. It was just a casual, instinctive reaction and he smiled rather shyly. When she came back I asked her if she was happy, being married this third time. She said that she was in love with him but not quite in the way she'd perhaps wanted. That there were so many questions left unanswered. The only time she had any real answers was when things went against the grain. But he was a lovely man. Her eyes went soft as she looked at him standing over by the bookcase looking closely at the negro sculptures, and she said: "My father thought the Americans were an uncivilized people. But they know all there is to know about the history of America, everything." He felt her looking at him and knew that we were talking about him. He turned around and gave her a smile. Then he pointed at the negro sculptures and said: "Nice dolls." I saw that Olga was a little embarrassed because that wasn't exactly how one described those things. But when I talked about them and called them dolls too she gave me a very sweet smile. She said it was so difficult with the language; she might be fluent enough in English but if she wanted to say something complicated or explain something about herself she often didn't bother. It was just too much trouble. A while ago when someone had played the wrong card at bridge, she had said: "That mouse will have a tail." They had all burst into laughter. She still didn't know if it was because English had no such expression or because of the situation. It made him laugh all over again and he put his arm around her when he sat down beside her. She said it was so nice to think that with him she would never have to stay in one place. That she would always wander from one place to the next. They would rent a furnished house everywhere they went. Carry nothing with them but a few suitcases. Live among furniture that belonged to nobody or everybody. And she told me excitedly that before they went to the Arabian Gulf he was going to show her all of America. From Nebraska to Texas. And in the spring they were going on a honeymoon to Mexico. A delayed honeymoon. When I got the box with photos out she jumped up and pushed me back with them. He wanted to see them but she wouldn't let him. She said they didn't have time to go through them now, they had to go, there were still so many things to do these last few days before their departure. And she promised that if it was at all possible they would call in again. But I knew for certain that she would stay away because of those photos. She wouldn't let him see her as she used to be. He had to love her as she was now. And I was right because for several months I had no news from her at all. Then I got a postcard from America with a coloured picture of a house with the wrought iron balustrades of New Orleans. The message on the back was as hard to decipher as her loveletters used to be: *This is a very big country. In the centre of some kind of jungle in Florida we were caught in a rainstorm. The road was full of tree branches that break because the moss on them grows too heavy with rain.* As I read that I was reminded of the first time I met her, driving over that road full of branches broken off by the frost. *We had to leave the car and clear the road several times. And we saw a tortoise cross over. Just like that in the wilderness! Best regards! Olga.* That spring I received another postcard with a The Troubles with Harry-like autumn landscape on it. AUTUMN IN THE FEATHER RIVER COUNTRY OF CALIFORNIA. No details, just greetings. But from Mexico she sent me a short letter. A fortnight after Easter. She wrote that surrounded by the house-high cactuses and the burros she had suddenly thought of me. She had seen a bumble-bee and a butterfly sitting on a sort of thistle together and it had conjured up the Verkade Biscuit Album, *The Flowers and their Friends* that I had. She also wrote that the local people had a horrible custom. On Easter Saturday they burnt Judas dolls everywhere, dolls large as life made especially for Easter. As they drove through a village where the dolls had been set alight, her husband had said it was just like the Ku Klux Klan. And how she longed for Alkmaar in that heat. For the green meadows and the water. After the letter came a further trickle of postcards. From Manzanillo. (A colourful fish-market with huge turtles.) Vera Cruz, Yucatan. (A temple dedicated to a people eater, a cannibal, she said on the card.) Each time I found one of her cards in my letterbox I couldn't work for the rest of the day, beset by melancholy and a lack of purpose. Perhaps it would have been better if she hadn't come to see me and I had never heard from her again. Because it was starting to look a lot like the lousy motto those American cupcakes had once pinned to the wall of their room: THERE IS NOTHING SADDER THAN ASSOCIATIONS HELD TOGETHER BY NOTHING BUT THE GLUE OF POSTAGE STAMPS. It seemed as if my far-away darling could feel my thoughts as there was nothing for the next half year or so. Until Christmas of that year. Another card came. But from the other side of the globe almost. With a map of the Arabian Gulf. And a ribbon over a very blue sea that said: GREETINGS FROM TRUCIAL STATES. In the bottom left hand corner was an Arabian with a camel, on the right a palm-treed oasis. A series of red dots ran along the coast: drilling installations sucking at the country like mosquitos. On the back, with an arrow pointing to the purple stamp which had a sheikh parading in a green oval, she had written: *A look at the real Sheikh of Araby, the one you had on the Benny Goodman record when I first knew you.* She also wrote that she'd been scared of the veiled women when she first arrived. And the camels and the rats came right up to the house in the morning and in the evening. And they had visited an area just vacated by locusts. It was laid bare and everything was sticky and had a bitter smell. And how much the men looked at her, making her husband jealous. She ended her note with the promise to write a letter when there weren't so many new things to look at. And I got it. At the start of the new year. Three pages of it: *Winter here means sand storms and people with colds. Yesterday we had about ten drops of rain. We live in the centre of the city across from a mosque, in a block of modern flats between all /the Arabian hovels. At the moment it is Ramadan, the Muslim fast. No one eats or drinks from sunrise to sundown and smoking isn't allowed. Even we are forbidden to eat or smoke in the street or in the car. If they catch you, you get sent to prison. At half past five when the sun goes down they fire two cannons as an aperitif, food appears from nowhere and the singing (wailing as far as I'm concerned) in the mosque begins. This praying takes hours and sounds terribly un-musical. It took me a while to tell it apart from the tomcats that wander outside the house. At three o'clock in the morning I sit in bed stiff with fear. At that time you're warned of the last chance to stuff yourself. It's done by means of two ʲ ums played in a way that would even terrify Hitler. They go through all the streets and you expect your murderer at any moment. This fasting lasts four weeks.* She also wrote that the people hunted doves. Of the same variety we used to keep. At first she was outraged. But later on she had eaten them with a lot of garlic and lemon. It seemed she wanted to needle me because she added that she'd eaten sheeps brains and even, unknowing, their eyes. It had been difficult to admit they did taste excellent. Her letter ended on this note. She had saved the best for last. The very last. Because I had no more letters from her, or cards with GREETINGS FROM TRUCIAL STATES!

Fuck Me I'm Desperate

Eight months after the sheep-brains and sheep-eyes she suddenly walked in. The house was open and she knocked on my studio door. As I opened it I thought she was going to collapse into my arms, her legs were so shaky. A pair of sunglasses pushed into her hair made her look like a mud skipper. She was pale as a ghost and a big red scar ran along her right jaw. But when I took her arm to guide her inside, my concern plainly showing, she pushed me away sharply and said there was nothing the matter with her. She just couldn't get used to the foul Dutch climate. I assumed she was on leave but once she'd settled down with her coffee she told me her mother had flown out to bring her home. Olga had sent a telegram and the bitch had lost no time dragging her suckling back to the nest. I couldn't take my eyes off her scar, that raw pink flesh with brown spots. But I didn't ask her what had happened. I could be fairly certain she was going to tell me about it. And she did. Even when they were travelling through the United States there had been difficulties. The other ovary began to play up, became infected and her innards were in a complete turmoil. She had a five-day period every fortnight. And she was in terrible pain when he slept with her. He had been very tender and understanding. But once they were in their flat among the hovels of the Arabians that had changed. She said it was the climate and the boredom that eventually drove everyone berserk. When he came back from an inspection tour of the drilling installations and she couldn't oblige, he'd tank up at the American Club. Downing a whole bottle of bourbon in an hour. And when he rolled home he parked himself on the edge of the bed slapping his mobile flat feet together for hours on end. It drove her crazy. Everything did after a while. The heat. The abominable habits of the people that encircled them. Of whom they knew nothing. She had been friendly with an older woman, the wife of one of her husband's colleagues. Quite a sane woman, who read books on theosophy but never talked about it. But all of a sudden she began pushing notes under the doors of the women in the flat when the men were away. Notes with: *Master your passions! Strive for conscious Union with the Universal! Passion disturbs the Harmony of the Universe! Love is the joining Force of the Great Universal Magnet!* And similar nonsense. And one night she ended up taking her lipstick to the walls of the stairway, the corridors and even the lift-shaft to write: FUCK ME I'M DESPERATE in bright red letters a foot high. Then she ran away from the flat in just her panties and a bra. They had found her in the slums the next morning, sleeping in the gutter. Fucked dry. The inside of her thighs raw. Whole tribes must have gone over her. Instead of seeing her to a hospital, the rest of them had scraped those burning red letters off the walls and hastily covered the places with whitewash so it would be dry before the men came home. Then Olga's tale drifted back to her Humphrey Bogart. As screwing became almost impossible his jealousy grew, and the dark, handsome Arabs looked at her so hard it made your nipples rise. And she looked back at them. What else was there? She had to work it off with looks and flirting. Because there was nothing to do but a bit of eating and a bit of drinking. And life is short. So when her husband was away on one of his two-week inspection tours she some-

146

times went out with an Arab. Just for the drive in his car and maybe a bit of necking. But she'd never been really unfaithful, she said. She couldn't, even had she wanted to. And then one day as she was sitting in a cafe with her Arab friend, her husband walked in when he should have been a hundred miles away. Someone must have squealed on her. He looked calm and restrained as he made his way over to them but in the next moment he had pulled her from behind the table and ˏslugged her in the face. Her Arab friend wouldn't stand for it. Threateningly he'd leapt up to fight, flailing his arms and ducking back to take running jumps at her husband. But it had just been for show. The vain flutter of a little bantam. Her husband flattened that Arab with three blows and knocked him out cold when he scrambled up again. The Arab in his magnificent dress lay on the ground like a rag as her husband suddenly faced her with a gun. Afterwards she hadn't known if he meant to shoot her or was simply forcing her to come with him. People began to pull at him from all sides. Then the shot had gone off. She'd felt nothing. Just a warm, tingling sensation. There was no feeling at all, she said, as she ran her hand over the scar. She could hold a burning cigarette to it. She thought her husband probably had some kind of brain damage. Always under that burning sun, and all that liquor. To make matters worse he had bought a chameleon. From a merchant who brought it in from Madagascar. It horrified her, that beast in its tank in her sitting room where she was alone with it all day. And those eyes, following her everywhere. Just like being constantly spied on through the keyhole. It fed on cockroaches. If her husband was drinking and playing cards with his friends and he saw a cockroach crawl along the wall, he couldn't be bothered to catch it himself. It was up to her to cut off a piece of tape and stick the cockroach to the wall. Because she wouldn't have touched those things for all the tea in China. He'd just point and call: "Cockroach, cockroach!" At night in bed, when she couldn't sleep from the heat, she imagined hearing the little legs of those imprisoned horrors scratching on the plaster. He took them down in the morning and threw them in with the chameleon. And she didn't mind that creature eating the cockroaches. But the sounds it produced doing it! Awful! When I asked her how things had gone for her husband after that, she said that he was most likely in prison or in an institution. When the police led him away after the investigation the last thing he'd called out to her was that he would always know where to find her. He had looked at her with a set face and said grimly: "Olga, you'd better look over your shoulder." It put the fear of God into her and she sent her mother a telegram to come and get her. Now she was back in Alkmaar. Among those wet and soggy meadows. And she had a bursting headache from the fog, the same headache she used to get from the scorching Arabian heat. I said that at least she had her freedom again. She flared out at me: "But I don't want to be free at all. I am terribly unhappy that way." Then she dropped her head in her hands, pushing her hair into a fluffy disorder. She sat very still. I looked at her pearl-shell painted nails on the oldish white hands and the red hair that had the same dull and faded look. And it took a great effort not to sit down beside her, throw my arm around her and have a good cry together. Into the silence she said, in a flat voice as if talking to herself: "Ah, I rushed straight into it as usual. I thought, this man will show me around the world,

148

and I've already forgotten most of it. Except the beastly things. The heat and the rotten insects. And my body playing up; you have to drag that with you wherever you go. I tell you I'm not at all satisfied with the life I have led up to now. Not at all. Sometimes I wonder if I should go to a psychiatrist. I can't figure it out. If you keep your feelings buried you just don't know what's going on in the end. I have pushed it all down. Us too. Until you showed me those photos just before I left, when it rose to the surface." She got up and walked around. Suddenly she stopped and pointed at the floor and said that she had seen that floor area as clear as glass during the worst of the heat. How we had sat there listening to the two Benny Goodman records when she first came home with me. What I had said to her when we were necking: "And now I should like to discharge my precious seed." And how frightened she had been. She broke into a hoarse laughter, stretched herself, pressed her hands to her stomach and asked if I didn't think her breasts were getting bigger again. She said she used a breast ointment. She had brought home pots and pots of it. From Abu Dhabi. She had enough to last her to her sixtieth, she said, laughing. When you rubbed it on it gave you a warm tingly feeling as if you were lying under an electric blanket. The skin went red. And when that had gone you could see that they really had swollen. Her husband used to laugh at her. He said it didn't help at all and that he didn't care if it did or not. That it was common hormone cream from the States which the Arabs put in their own little pots and disguised with mysterious labels. I wondered what she was fishing for. Should I be asking to see her breasts so she could have my word for it that they were back to when I knew them? Or was she just chattering on like a

149

chicken with its head cut off, without any real motive. Whatever it was, a reconciliation on the basis of breast cream wasn't laid away for us. She was on to another topic by this time. America. Where she had a good time nevertheless. Some days she'd eaten as many as five lobsters and once, along a road stretching through miles of prairie, they saw a bunch of cowboys slaughtering a cow. They had left the car and gone over to watch the animal being hacked to pieces and roasted on the spot. They stayed all evening. It had been just like *River of No Return* with Marilyn Munroe she had seen with me in the distant past. The next morning she could still feel the heat of the fire on her cheeks, she had been so close. It was a crazy country. In one town the nipples of the girls that served you almost hung in your plate while in the next one along they painted even the chrome on their cars black and you had to hide the nicotine stains on your fingers or you weren't welcome. One evening when her husband was doing a hundred miles an hour because they were exhausted and the nearest hotel was a hundred and ten miles away, a blue flashing light suddenly appeared beside them. A roar: "Didn't you see our radar?" A big brute of a policeman in black leather. But after she had given him a pair of miniature wooden shoes he was wax in her hands. His ancestors had come from Holland. And there was no more talk of fines. Then she switched back to the Freak Show she saw with me when we met the second time, at the fair on the Nieuwmarkt. She had always remembered the wax woman lashed to a torture pole with a weight around her waist. Red streaks ran down her legs and there was blood at her mouth. She had felt like that woman when her husband, the second one, had said to her once: "You're as proud as Joan of Arc but not as strong," before he took her by force. It had sickened her. Just as nauseating as the time I scrunched those jellyfish on the beach of Ameland with a spade. Even though she knew they were already dead. But they had quivered in the wind, making it seem they were still alive. She suddenly had her fill of recalling the past. Her purpose in coming to Amsterdam was to see a gynaecologist. For the rot in her belly as well as for that agonizing headache. And before she left she said she was the exact opposite of the woman who had written "Fuck me I'm desperate" on the walls. She was desperate too, but she wanted to yell: "For God's sake leave me alone!"

Rosa Turbinata

When her mother phoned me not very long after, it immediately shocked through me that there must be something wrong with Olga. Her voice carried a sham condolence—to leave me in no doubt that she was being strong and brave and knew how to control herself. She said that Olga's headaches had grown worse and worse. One night she found her unconscious in the lavatory. She had been lying there for hours. As their doctor couldn't find anything wrong with her they took photos of her head in the hospital in Amsterdam. And even before she went back for the results, they telephoned for her to be taken up. She was to have a brain operation immediately. They sawed a trapdoor in the side of her head and took out a tumour the size of a bar of soap. But they had to leave the roots because they had grown into the brain. And taking them out would have paralyzed her. She was now having daily ray treatment and the people in the hospital were very hopeful. Olga had been asking for me and she was phoning me to see if I could look in from time to time. Because she was the only one who came and she couldn't very well make the trip into Amsterdam every day. As she was telling me all this a dizziness seemed to come over me. An inability to grasp the seriousness of the situation. For I saw Olga floating in a glassy light, her hair the length of Botticelli's *Venus*. Just as beautiful as in the past. Restored to her former glory. Not until I had put the phone down—after firmly settling the hours that I would visit, because I had not the least intention of running into that varmint, and I told her so—did I feel the strange tightness of my eyes and face. All she had done in the last few years, from her sudden flight from me to the cockroaches of the Arabian Gulf, might have been caused by the colourless bulb in her head, biting its greedy roots into her brain. I recalled her curious staring spells before she left me for ever. On reflection it was as if she'd been listening to what was taking place inside. And then fled in panic from something she didn't understand but that she carried with her. Everywhere. Inescapable as a shadow. After that phone call I immediately rang a friend who was an intern at the hospital. "The lovely redhead of a few years ago? What a shame." He said that nothing could be done. He might as well give it to me straight, since she was out of my life anyway. They had a bash at controlling it with radiation but it was a stay of execution. Those roots didn't go away. With one it might be five years before that lot began growing again, with another it was a matter of months. He told me what I already knew. That she was done for. And I repeated to myself in nervous confusion and the tears streaming down my face: "You're going to die, Olga. You're going to die." The following afternoon I went to see her. She was in a small private room. The first thing I noticed when I walked in was a big window with a lot of park-like trees behind it. Softened by the texture of the window screen, capturing the light in a golden glow it was like a Gobelin. She was lying in the bluish shade inside the little room and outside the sun shone. I laid the roses at the bottom of her bed and walked up to her. She put out her hand. It felt slack and watery and her face, too, was flabby. It made her eyes seem smaller. The left side of her head was shorn. There was hardly anything in the way of scars. Some small reddish lines. You could only tell by the trembling of the skin that there was no bone behind it. The hair that remained was short and full of bald patches. She drew her fingers through it nervously and said, while looking at herself in a pocket mirror, that she might lose her hair altogether. That's what the doctor had said. The X-ray treatments did it. But later it would grow back to normal and you wouldn't be able to see the scar. She tried to laugh and said she now had a skull with a door. That they were putting back the piece of bone later on. It was being kept on ice downstairs. It was such a peculiar feeling. That there was a piece of her somewhere else. It kept reminding her of the Anton Pieck print on the cover of *The Wind from the Mountains* by Trygve Gulbranssen in her mother's bookcase. A glacier-like wall of ice with a skull drawn in it. She had felt that icy coldness in her head. In the opening. When

I sat down beside the bed she said how well I looked and I hated myself for being such a healthy bastard. Healthy and incapable of doing anything for her. She said that when she first looked outside she'd thought, what beautiful light green flowers on those trees. And she'd lain there wondering what that could be, light green flowers. Mysterious. Until the nurse told her those were chestnuts on the trees. There was something wrong with her eyes all the same. The writing on the picture of the rose on the wall opposite had been quite clear before. *Rosa turbinata*. But now all she could see were grey blobs. She wasn't allowed to read: it was too tiring they said. But last week her mother had a woman's journal with her. She had hidden it under the blankets and when she tried to read it later on she kept having to go back to the beginning because after a few sentences she had forgotten what she read. Sometimes she couldn't even recognize the pattern of the words and had to spell them out like a school child. Suddenly she asked how the cat was doing. I didn't only tell her how the cat was doing now but also how she had been since the time Olga left. That at first she walked to the door every time she heard high heels outside. That she had looked for Olga all over the house. She started to cry and said that the kitten she delivered herself was the only one that had really been hers. She'd been terribly upset when it had to go. I moved my chair closer to the bed, put my arm around her shoulder and said that when she was better we would go and see it together. She nodded, but kept crying. I laid my hand on her wet cheek and pressed her head to me. We stayed that way until the nurse came in, cheerfully, as if it was a maternity case and said that the visiting hour was over. And this is how, a few times a week, I spent a couple of hours beside her in that last half year of her life. And through that window with the screen that wasn't removed in the winter the two of us saw the trees go yellow, saw the snow fall. But by the time everything went green again I had to tell her about it. By then she was almost completely blind. At first I would usually find her calm and serene. She'd have a very clear recall of the past. Being on a bench in the Vondelpark together, sucking honey from weigelias and how there'd been great wads of black dog hair in the litter box beside us. That the asphalt was always wet with dew when we came from night concerts and that once, sitting on the terrace of the restaurant in the Zoo we saw a herring gull swallow a sparrow whole when it came too close to him. She still saw the little bird struggle through that gullet. Horrible. One time she mentioned she had bought a small statue for me from a dig in Mexico. Terra cotta. A couple making love, with the earth still sticking to it. She had left it somewhere in a hotel in San Diego. But later on she often behaved like a whining child. She'd make me feel her front teeth several times in an afternoon as she thought they were loose. She'd want to send me off in the middle of the visiting hour to get her a bag of Turkish Delight, the only kind of sweets she dare eat with her loose front teeth. Or she wanted me to help her put a jig-saw puzzle together all afternoon, a puzzle with an autumn landscape of the same exuberance as the postcard she sent me from California. Every time I found a couple of good pieces and she tried them on the puzzle she took them off again and said they weren't the right ones, they didn't fit. There was something malicious about her then. And I had to be very tactful in giving her the fitting pieces again and make her think she had found them herself. Or else she became more and more obstinate and nibbled and niggled at the landscape until we were back where we started. Before the end of that year she was completely bald. It really quite suited her the way she looked now. With that bulbous swollen face. A mentally defective earth mother who appears to be smiling because she can barely see. But she couldn't stand the thought of it. She didn't know what to do with herself. Every time I came she could have pulled the pillow down over her head from embarrassment. That's why, after consulting the doctor, I bought her a wig. I borrowed six hundred guilders which I wasn't able to pay back until a year after her death. It was a bit brighter red than her hair used to be. She was enthralled. The first afternoon she wore it she kept brushing her hands over her head. But it looked awful on her. A nightmare. Because you could no longer tell she was sick. As though she'd always looked like this. Like a swollen malignant fairy tale princess. One of Cinderella's bad-tempered, treacherous stepsisters. And when it was on crooked she looked so silly I could have laughed and wept at the same time. She began to tell me things I thought she must be inventing. About her American husband blackening her eye on a regular basis. Every time they'd been out and he thought she had flirted with someone else he knocked her on the head at home, in the hall. That's why she was so sick now. And he always took down the mileage of the car if he had to be away for a while. Then she had to account for herself when he came back. And one time when they were both drunk he had undressed her and put iceblocks in her cunt. She could have jumped out of the window on those Arabian hovels below it was so hot and it itched so. Sometimes she told stories about me as if she had quite forgotten that it was me sitting there. How I made her cycle beside me for hours. Until she was so tired that she fell, bicycle and all, in the grass on the side of the road. And I always made her steal roses out of parks and the thorns made her fingertips bleed. She had been scared stiff they'd catch her at it one day. But as time went by even the lying and the fantasy stopped. All I could do then was read her something. Anything, nonsense from a woman's journal. It didn't matter where I started. When I stopped a moment, she some times spoke. It became more and more disjointed but there were times that I knew she wanted to say things about the past. When it registered who I was. And one time she said, out of the blue: "When there's a cold spell in the middle of August everything becomes chaotic." Not long after, it all stopped. Her sight was gone. She could barely talk. Her eyes bulged out as if they were being pushed from behind. She grew fatter and puffier. Still I kept bringing her flowers. More because of the nurse than for her. It would have been indecent to stop just because she couldn't see them any more. Such a stifling, inconsolable sadness came over me as I walked into her room that I wanted to be like Oliver Hardy and bowl in with his bashful and clumsy cheer yelling: "Aloha babe!" And then jump through that glass and that screen with my roses for a sail and float away over the budding chestnuts with her. Changed back, by magic, into the girl of my dreams. When I came one afternoon in the first days of Spring, she was dead. She had died the previous evening. The doctor said I shouldn't ever reproach myself. I had done what I could. They had admired me for always being on time and never leaving sooner than I had to. Even when she could no longer have known I was there. He said that it had meant very much to her. That I had made her deeply happy with that wig, because when she died she had pressed it with both her hands to her head. After I had looked at her for the last time—no more repulsive than she had been of late—and the doctor walked down the corridor with me, he asked if he should keep the wig for me as she was being boxed straight away and sent to the Velzen crematorium. I said that she was to wear it. That she had wanted it that way.